Oedipus Trilogy

Oedipus Trilogy

King Oedipus
Oedipus at Colonos
Antigone

A Version by
Stephen Spender

Random House New York

Library of Congress Cataloging in Publication Data
Spender, Stephen, 1909–
Oedipus trilogy.
1. Oedipus (Greek mythology)—Drama. 2. Antigone
(Legendary character)—Drama. I. Sophocles. Selections.
English. 1985. II. Title.
PR6037. P4703 1985   822'.912   84-45766
0-394-54483-8

Manufactured in the United States of America
2 3 4 5 6 7 8 9

To Francis Bacon

CONTENTS

INTRODUCTION

The play in three acts that follows is based on *Oedipus Rex*, *Oedipus at Colonos* and *Antigone* of Sophocles. It is intended primarily for stage performance but also to be read. I wrote it in the first place because in 1981 Mr Gordon McDougall, at that time director of the Oxford Playhouse, invited me to write a version in which the three plays could be produced as one play in three acts, to be performed within the space of a single evening.

The draft I then wrote was performed at the Oxford Playhouse for two weeks in March 1983 and, after that, by the same company for a week at the Arts Theatre in Cambridge. The performance lasted approximately three and a half hours. The present version is considerably longer, but it can, of course, be cut. I attended several rehearsals and about five performances at Oxford. Doing so gave me the opportunity, rare for a poet, of hearing words I had written spoken by others.

What I heard then seemed a draft for a poetic drama which remained to be written. On the basis of this draft, I spent a year writing the present work, which has very little in common with it.

My aim is to present in very clear language, written to be spoken, or to be read as if the reader were hearing it spoken, the story of the house of Labdacus in bare outline, portraying the characters and choruses.

When I was writing the Oxford Playhouse version I consulted many translations, several of them in verse. But in this final version I have relied only on the prose translation of R. C. Jebb, in *The Complete Greek Drama*, edited by Whitnet J. Oates and Eugene O'Neill (Random House).

I have improvised freely only in the speeches of shepherds,

guards and a few passages of line-by-line dialogue
(stichomythia) where it seemed important, above all else, to
convey the swiftness of repartee.

I should admit at once that my knowledge of Greek is limited
to what little I have retained throughout my life after studying
it for two years when I was in the sixth form at University
College School, London, in the late twenties. I learned then the
role of Apollo in the *Eumenides* for a school performance. I
retain an almost hallucinatory memory of the dynamic gestures
of rhythm and imagery in the Greek, and an ideal of clarity
working within the complex mythology.

The basic rhythmic unit here is the iambic pentameter –
sometimes regular (as in the last great speech of Oedipus in
Oedipus at Colonos, when his life is moving towards its close),
sometimes quite irregular. A few of Creon's speeches are
broken-up prose. In general, I have tried to make the language
capable of being spoken either as prose or as verse. The metre
is, as it were, available to the performer, as he or she requires
it. There are, of course, passages in which emphatic rhythm is
essential – the speeches made by Oedipus after he has torn out
his eyes, and his outbursts in the second play.

Some speeches are in prose where I thought situation and
character required this. For instance, the central scene of *Oedipus
Rex* in which Oedipus relates to Jocasta the story of his youth in
Corinth and of how he killed a stranger who approached him
threateningly on the road near Phosis. For the drama here lies in
the pressure of the factual narrative on the language (as though
Oedipus were reading from a book inscribed on his memory)
unimpassioned by his usual hyperbole.

I was doubtful whether to write the opening speech of
Oedipus in prose or in verse – at Oxford I had it in prose – but
finally decided on verse because here Oedipus is already
offering himself to the Thebans in the role of saviour.
Moreover, it seemed important to establish at the outset the

basic rhythmic unit of the play.

Besides making cuts and transpositions, writing the trilogy as a three-acter meant finding a unity absent from these three separate plays about the fall of the house of Labdacus. No continuous line of development runs through the trilogy, which leads to a climax bringing all the threads of narrative together. They were written at very different periods in the life of Sophocles – which would, in any case, prevent their having sustained any consistent dramatic unity. *Antigone* was first (about 442 BC); *Oedipus Rex*, second; and, last, *Oedipus at Colonos*, written in the poet's extreme old age (reputedly when he was 84) and first performed after his death.

Oedipus Rex and *Oedipus at Colonos* bear a relationship to each other which is almost that of opposites – Yeatsian antimonies. In the first play Oedipus discovers that he is guilty of murdering his father, King Laius, and of marrying his mother, Jocasta. He himself is the man who brought the plague upon Thebes. In the second play, he acquits himself of both crimes on the grounds that he was the unwitting instrument of supernatural forces that wished to destroy him. The first play is permeated with the feeling of an ancestral curse, a kind of original sin, the second play that of discovered innocence.

The difference of attitude in the two plays seems as striking as that between Old and New Testaments. Note that in both plays Oedipus is his own judge and jury, convicting himself in the first, acquitting himself in the second. On one level, the Oedipus plays seem to be about individual conscience – whether Oedipus feels himself guilty or innocent. The Chorus is not his judge, nor his jury. They are commentators, advisers, witnesses and gossips, sometimes mocking. In their lyrical *intermezzi* they draw general conclusions, moralize and underline fate, but they do not pass sentence on Oedipus. At the end of *Oedipus Rex* they simply note his fall. Nor can the gods who caused him such suffering in the first play be seen to acquit him of guilt in the second. At the end of *Oedipus at Colonos* they draw him up into their reconciling harmonies whereby he is redeemed – on account of his suffering, not on account of his self-declared innocence.

In my mental picture of an ideal production of *Oedipus Trilogy*, I see the setting of the first play as rocky, sombre, almost colourless; that of the second play (*Oedipus at Colonos*) as sunlit, full of colour, white with gleaming columns, green with olive groves, blue and white-waved for the sea, white and dappled for horses; that of the third, reverting to the primitivism of the first: stony city walls, the rocks of Antigone's living tomb, the tawny desert plain on to which the corpse of Polyneices is thrown, to be the prey of dogs and vultures. The interior of Creon's palace should be barbarian and garish.

In the first play, Oedipus, in the prime of life (his early thirties, approximately the same age as Laius when he was murdered), is a man of passionate action following a fixed course in pursuit of Laius' murderer – without giving a moment's thought to the consequences. In the second play, he is an old man, blind, a wandering beggar, incapable of action, but capable of words as violent and intemperate as were once his deeds.

There is no contradiction inherent in *Oedipus at Colonos* in Oedipus declaring himself innocent of the crimes of which he first found himself guilty. All he has done is to change his attitude towards the supernatural forces. When he first realized that he was regicide, patricide and committer of incest with his mother, he condemned himself. But later, on reflection, he came to think that after all he was not guilty – merely an instrument of those forces. He proclaims his innocence with the same fervour – ferocity almost – as formerly he had proclaimed his guilt.

Although there is no real contradiction involved in Oedipus' change of attitude, there is nevertheless glaring contradiction between the account he gives in *Oedipus at Colonos* of his staying on at Thebes after putting out his eyes, and what the audience has seen – his being driven out at his own request. True, when Oedipus asks Creon to drive him out Creon replies that the oracle must be consulted, but he seems to withdraw this objection. Moreover, the expulsion of Oedipus corroborates Teiresias' prediction – Teiresias is the great repository of sacred truth throughout the trilogy, and cannot make a false prophecy.

Oedipus declares in the second play that he was not driven out of Thebes, but stayed there a while, thinking things over, and concluding that, after all, he was not guilty and, therefore, could live out the remainder of his days in Thebes. He now says that only when he had come to this decision did Creon drive him out. Doubtless some tinkering with the myth is necessary to make Creon the unmitigated villain of *Oedipus at Colonos*. The second play hinges on Creon's brutal attempt to carry Oedipus back to Thebes, where his presence is now seen as insurance against defeat in war with Athens.

Rather than disguise or suppress the contradiction, I have brought it into the open. I make the Chorus challenge this version of the past. They point out that he himself asked to be driven from Thebes. The contradiction becomes an aspect of the character of Oedipus. For the only unifying interpretation of these three plays lies in the psychology of the protagonists. It is entirely in character for Oedipus to contradict himself. He is given to hyperbole and exaggeration. His accusations against Creon in *Oedipus Rex* are so intemperate and so unsubstantiated we scarcely believe them: only Creon's behaviour in *Antigone* lends them retrospective point. They tell us more about the violence of Oedipus than they do about Creon. In the second play, too, Oedipus's outbursts against his sons are in general justified but

extravagant in particulars. It is beside the point to call them
effete Egyptians who sit around doing embroidery while their
women do the work. Creon is perfectly aware that once
Oedipus lets rip he will show himself demonstrably unfair – an
accuser whose charges rebut themselves.

Oedipus is not an objective witness to fact, even though he
is set on tracking down the murderer of Laius. He has no
forensic gifts. His quest obeys the oracle. He must follow the
evidence wherever it may lead – even if to his own destruction
(and he makes allowance for this possibility from the first). The
guardian of the truth is Teiresias who (together with Jocasta)
tries to protect Oedipus from discovering it.

To a modern audience it may seem that Oedipus is in search
of the truth about himself. A consequence incidental to the
search for the murderer may, he thinks, be the discovery that
he is son of one of the shepherds who saved his life when he
was a baby. He is perfectly prepared to accept this. He has to
know who he is. He sneers at Jocasta, assuming that she
objects to his enquiries because she does not wish to discover
that she is married to serf stock.

I suspect that Wagner had Oedipus in mind when he created
the character of Siegfried. Similarly, when he wrote the scene
in *Rheingold* where the giant Fafner seizes Freia, he may have
been remembering the scene in which Creon (in *Oedipus at
Colonos*) lays hold first on Ismene and then Antigone, whom he
carries off. Whether or not I am right about this, Siegfried
throws light on the youthful Oedipus who killed the traveller
who pushed him aside on the highway. Is not his behaviour
like that of the young Siegfried who goes around slaying
dragons, dwarfs, all and sundry without the least
compunction? Both feel completely innocent (and with no one
to dispute this) until one day they are trapped in a catastrophic
situation. And, even then, Oedipus remains innocent, the
unwitting agent of the malevolence of Apollo. So far from

[16]

being guilty, Oedipus is incapable of guilt: it is his very
innocence that makes him the instrument of the curse laid on
his family, the vengefulness of the god. When Oedipus relates
to Jocasta the story of the traveller and his retinue at the
crossroads, of how he killed all but one, is there not a certain
Siegfried-like boastfulness about him? This is one of the
subtlest touches in the first play – the small boy boasting of his
prowess to his wife – who, at this moment, is unconsciously
cast in the role of mother – which is what she really is.

If the three plays are treated as one, Creon becomes the
dominating figure in all three. He is materialistic, bureaucratic
– the world that is always with us. He reveals different aspects
of his character in each play so that, more than any other role,
his imposes on the actor the necessity of discovering a unifying
character. Consistent throughout is his assured sense of his
own authority. From his first entrance he shows that contempt
for his brother-in-law Oedipus with which the man of affairs
regards the dreamer. In saying that he is the uncrowned power
behind the throne (which he shares jointly with Oedipus and
Jocasta) he implicitly asserts that he is the only capable member
of the triumvirate. He watches Oedipus and waits for him to
pass. (He must always have the air of watching and waiting
until the moment when he attains the crown.) In *Oedipus at
Colonos*, although Creon has superseded Oedipus, he is still
only regent, the throne being shared first by Eteocles and
Polyneices, and later, presumably, after the flight of Polyneices
to Argos, by Eteocles alone. Perhaps Creon's arrogant bullying
in the second play is due to his frustrated ambition. He wishes
to make a show of power.

He becomes king at the opening of *Antigone*. Here his
triumphant entry belies his earlier claim that he was content to
be the power behind the throne. I would have him wearing his
crown, and perhaps attired in gold. Although he retains his
capacity to govern rationally, power does go to his head: he is

not so much unjust to Antigone as self-indulgent. He allows his anti-feminism and his contempt for those who introduce religion into politics to influence him. He is legalistic and bureaucratic, proud and pompous and downright cruel but he is never irrational – except perhaps when, furious with Teiresias, he blasphemes against the gods.

His opening speech in *Antigone*, however cliché-ridden and full of mixed metaphor, shows him a man of principle with a carefully thought-out position and policies. He is a sincere patriot, though for him Thebes is himself. As a responsible ruler his attitude towards Antigone is justified. It is intolerable that Polyneices, a traitor and rebel, should be given burial rights equal with those given to Eteocles. (We may bear in mind here that Oedipus would have thrown out both these scoundrelly sons to be devoured by dogs and vultures.) Creon knows what is right and boasts that he knows. He cannot bear to be contradicted, least of all by idealists, poets, the young and incompetent. His misfortune is to deal with people like Antigone and Haemon. Creon's excesses are always the result of provocation by someone whom he considers unrealistic or irresponsible: by Oedipus, by Antigone, by Haemon, by Teiresias, even by the guard who arrests Antigone. Provoked, he can overstep margins – as he well knows. When he commits blasphemy, he does not want to offend the gods; he has simply lost all patience with Teiresias and his exclusive claim to represent the sublime authority of Olympus. He feels the impatience that the ruler of a country might feel for a particularly self-righteous moralizing archbishop. Warned by the Chorus, he recognizes his mistake almost immediately, and attempts to retreat. But he has gone too far: Teiresias really is a holy prophet; and Zeus was listening.

Creon's tragedy is not that of his whole moral and spiritual being, like that of Oedipus or Antigone, but that of a ruler intoxicated by power, who forgets the limits to that power laid

[18]

down by the gods. He has simply made a bad mistake, committed some monstrous indiscretion, and he knows this.

Antigone sets herself in line with the law of the gods, which is opposed to Creon's law. But perhaps she takes too much upon herself: in the context of the whole trilogy there is crude sense in Creon's comment in *Oedipus at Colonos* that she will be lucky if she finds a husband. Her betrothal to Haemon seems symbolic rather than real. There is no scene in which they are together. It expresses, though, the repressed half of her personality. At the end of *Oedipus at Colonos* she wants to follow her father to his tomb and at the beginning of *Antigone* she is seen as married to death. Her libations over the corpse of Polyneices are like some sombre celebration of her union with her dead brother and the ghosts of her parents.

But she has a split personality, and it is this that makes for her great dramatic interest. Her Self that is the Bride of Death – the Lord of the Dark Lake – projects an Opposite that enacts the role of the Bride of Life. It is almost as though with her flesh she is incestuously married to her brother and the house of Labdacus, and with her spirit or ghost betrothed to Haemon. When she is confronted by the reality of her entombment in the rocky cavern prescribed for her by Creon, she sees herself as ghost at her own bridal feast, sole mourner at her own funeral. She chooses martyrdom in the first part of the play that bears her name. In the second half, the side of her that is repressed bitterly regrets and resents the choice.

In her final speech there is a passage, spurious according to the scholars, in which, going back on all that she has stood for until then, she declares that if she had married and had children, she would have obeyed Creon's edict. It was only because Polyneices was her brother that she was bound to his death as to the doom of the house of Labdacus. Married, she would have escaped this bond of family. A husband killed, she would have found a new husband. With a family of her own,

[19]

her duty would have been to life not death.

The lines in which she expresses these sentiments are, of course, a big drop from the plane of grand self-dramatization on which she has been making her journey to her living tomb. Yet to the modern audience this may seem a shift from the falsely sublime to the psychologically true. The side of Antigone that wants to live turns accusingly against the side that has chosen death. The opposites confront each other.

Here, too, she is seen answering the Chorus, who have been mocking her precisely for her noble-mindedness. To be dramatically effective, the lines should be addressed directly to the Chorus. The argument may seem a bit tortuous: that if it were a husband and not a brother who lay out there unburied, she would go about the job of finding another husband. Yet they do express a truth and if the actress can reach to that feeling there is pathos in her *cri de coeur*. This leap from the heights of martyrdom into the absurdity of longing for ordinary life is poignant. 'Husband' becomes the name for all the life that she has renounced. Yet a husband would have been replaceable. Polyneices is irreplaceable because her parents are dead and he is her brother – flesh and blood of the house of Labdacus.

These lines are available to the performer, but can be omitted. One more available thing is a spurious interpolation of my own. At a friend's suggestion I have introduced the answer to the riddle of the Sphinx. Man is that creature which goes on all fours (as a baby), then on two legs (as a man) and then on three (as an ancient with a stick). I have done this partly because the riddle is several times referred to in the play, and the modern audience may not know the answer, partly because the image of one-legged, two-legged, three-legged animals seems a haunting reminder of the human condition, like Shakespeare's poor forked man in *King Lear*.

I have emphasized themes and symbols that unify all three

plays. The most obvious of these is blindness. Teiresias is blind, Oedipus blinds himself, Antigone is sentenced to be immured in a living tomb (a metaphor for her father's blindness), Creon acts blindly and goes down to his end lamenting his own blindness. There are moments when the machinery of the tragedy becomes, as it were, visible, like wheels turning that might be stopped. I give Jocasta the cry, 'Stop!' when she is imploring Oedipus not to go on in his hunt for the murderer of Laius and, again, to Ismene when she tries to stop Antigone from disobeying Creon's edict. Another theme that runs throughout the play is life-and-death incestuous relationships between parents and children. Oedipus, killing his father, marrying his mother, hating his sons, loving his daughters, is the pattern for all such entanglements. The attempt of Haemon to kill his father repeats the figure of Oedipus killing his father, which is reversed by Creon killing Haemon. Wicked as Polyneices is, the scene in which he pleads with Oedipus (his entreaties echoed by Antigone) has the pathos, in part, of an appeal against the pattern of hatred between father and son.

The questions that arise with regard to Jocasta are: how much did she know about the murder of Laius? How long ago must she have realized that Oedipus was her son? For the purpose of acting the role, the answer to the first question must be that when Oedipus told her about his meeting with the traveller whom he killed on the crossroads near Phosis, she must have realized that the man Oedipus killed was Laius. She panics at the idea of having to send for the servant to whom she had committed her baby child to be left on the bare hillside. But long before this she must have suspected at least that the scarred feet of her husband were those of the child who had been pinioned.

However much Jocasta knew or suspected, she is the very type of woman whose whole life is based on secrets that are

[21]

locked in her heart, secrets of time long past and buried so deep that she herself may have forgotten them: and, therefore, all the more terrible when they are unburied and spring back into recognition. When Teiresias complains to Oedipus that he has been sent for to answer questions about things that he had forgotten, he is speaking out of a darkness that is also the heart of Jocasta. For Jocasta they have become her deepest life, the 'deep declivities' of her own physical body, secrets of the womb. Her very existence depends on them being kept dark. Moreover she is guardian over them for the sake of Oedipus' life also.

To lay bare such secrets is, for Jocasta, madness and destruction. There are no circumstances in which she could understand that for Thebes to be saved from the plague, Oedipus must reveal them. The feminity of Jocasta is related to that of Teiresias, the man/woman who is led by a boy, guardian of the blind. (At the end of *Antigone*, Teiresias and his boy may appear almost as one person, a four-legged animal which recalls the riddle of the Sphinx.) The torment inflicted on Jocasta by Oedipus is of seeing him lay bare one of the past events on which their lives depend, like taking away layer on layer of bandages. She is the wife who sees a husband's unreflecting unprescient honesty destroy what are the very foundations of their happiness. The scene in which Oedipus does this inevitably reminds us of Ibsen.

The remaining characters are one-dimensional. Polyneices should be beautiful and damned and sweating, walking around the irresponsive statuesque figure of Oedipus. Theseus has poise, conscious magnanimity and speaks always in measured tones. He is a bit vain, too consciously virtuous. But at the end he has his moment of vision, like the disciple who is allowed to see the Ascension.

The greatest unifiers in the *Trilogy* are, of course, the Choruses: or, rather, the Chorus and the lyric poems that are

[22]

the Choruses. The Greek Chorus, with leader and diverse
followers, is not quite the passive spectator and occasional
commentator that it is reputed to be. Nor is it as remote from
us as we suppose. It is often like *Times* editorials, television
commentators, pollsters and the Voice of Democracy. In
Oedipus Rex the Chorus is monarchist, expressing the views of
a public that, though alarmed by the behaviour of the King, is
even more scared at the prospect of his removal. The attitude
of the Chorus to Oedipus in the first play is very much that of
the British public to Edward VIII at the time of the Abdication.
When Creon takes over and shows himself to be a ruler who
knows how to handle power, the Chorus is reassured. In
Oedipus at Colonos the Chorus, perhaps as much older than the
Chorus in the first play as Oedipus and Creon are older, shows
the fear and contempt for Oedipus that the organs of public
opinion would show any such revenant in such a situation.
Like the gutter press, it also demands of Oedipus that he
should tell them all the dirt about his colourful past, filling
their minds with evil. The Chorus sneers at Antigone when
she is being led to her tomb of rock. Though abject in the face
of the powerful when they are in office, the Chorus is smugly
moralizing about their fall.

The lyrics that form the Choruses are a very different matter
from the interventions of the Chorus. They are distillations of
religion or law, or reflections on the nature of existence. They
are charged by the dynamism of the surrounding action. They
can be lyrical *intermezzi* reaching beyond the action of the play,
though arising from it, like the poem sparked off by Oedipus
wondering who might be his father. They may be evocations of
place, like that of Colonos, or running comments on action
such as that of the battle taking place between Creon and
Theseus. Hamlet's prose monologue, 'What a piece of work is
a man' is in essence a Greek chorus.

The ending of *Antigone* presents difficulties. Sophocles intensifies the tragedy by introducing a new character, Euridice, Creon's queen, simply for the purpose of redoubling the tragic effect, like a composer introducing into the end of his symphony a row of instruments – perhaps double-basses – unplayed till then. To a modern audience it would seem absurd surely to have a character appear at the end of the play, only to commit suicide. I have tried to strengthen the ending by emphasizing the theme of blindness. The end of Creon is like history repeating itself, an echo of the death of Oedipus in the first play but doing so almost on the note of mockery. The House of Labdacus ends not with a bang but a whimper.

*   *   *

Besides thanking Mr Gordon McDougall for putting me on the track of this, I want to thank Mr Peter Porter for going through the early version with me and making many suggestions.

CHARACTERS

King Oedipus

OEDIPUS, King of Thebes
JOCASTA, his wife
CREON, brother of Jocasta
TEIRESIAS, a prophet
PRIEST
MESSENGER
HERDSMAN
ATTENDANTS
CHORUS OF THEBANS

Oedipus at Colonos

OEDIPUS
ANTIGONE
ISMENE ⎫ daughters of Oedipus
THESEUS, King of Athens
CREON, King of Thebes
POLYNEICES, son of Oedipus
STRANGER
ATTENDANTS
CHORUS OF ELDERS OF COLONOS

Antigone

ISMENE
ANTIGONE
CREONE
HAEMON
TEIRESIAS
MESSENGER
SOLDIER
ATTENDANTS
CHORUS OF THEBAN ELDERS

KING OEDIPUS

OEDIPUS

My children, last descendants of Cadmus,
Why do you stand there before me as suppliants
Waving wreathed olive branches?
Why does the whole city reek with incense?
Why do the streets of Thebes re-echo with
Prayers for your recovery from the plague?
Rumours have reached me of your plight.
So, not relying on reports from others,
I have come here to see things for myself.
I Oedipus, your king, most renowned of Thebans.
(*To a* PRIEST)
You, there, you old man, you are a priest.
You ought to know. What is the matter?
What are you afraid of? What do you want from me?
Rely on me to help you all I can
Indeed I would be made of stone, if I did not
Feel pity for suppliants such as these.

PRIEST

Oedipus, great king, as you can see
All the citizens of Thebes are now assembled –
Infants on all fours, men upright
On two legs, and the old, like myself with sticks,
Three-legged. Besides those here,
Others are in the market place or at
The shrine of Pallas Athene, praying.

[29]

CHORUS

(*Speaking in several voices*)

The city, as you see, is oppressed under
Ever-invading waves of death.
The blossoms wither on the fruit trees.
The cattle rot and fall down in the pastures.
Women are barren or bear stillborn children.
The plague's the only thing alive
Rushing with flaming torch from street to street
And tearing down the house of Cadmus.
Hell fattens on our groans and tears.

PRIEST

It is not as a god that we implore you
Oedipus, to rescue us, but as
The foremost of men. To us you are renowned
As he who came to Cadmus long ago
And freed us from the rank extortions
Of the contriving Sphinx.
You did this not through base self-interest
And not for payment but solely by
Making your will one with the god's.

CHORUS LEADER

Oedipus, once again we ask you
To save us either through the god's will or
Through being the first of men

CHORUS

(*Speaking in several voices*)

Let no one say you saved Thebes once before
But now in her hour of greater need desert her.
A king should not reign over a waste land.
A ship is nothing without crew and voyagers.

[30]

OEDIPUS

News of your sufferings already
Has reached me, O my children,
Your sorrows are written on my soul,
Know then, none of you suffers more than I do.
Each of you suffers for himself, but I
Being your king, suffer for you all,
I grieve for Thebes, for you, and for myself.
Your cries and lamentations do not wake
One who sleeps, but one who weeps all night –
Lying awake, puzzling out remedies,
Of all I've thought of, this seems wisest
Which I have acted on already,
I have sent Creon, my wife Jocasta's brother,
To the Pythian shrine, Apollo's oracle,
To ask the god by what means, act or word
We can save Thebes. And here he comes –
Creon, smiling, and his forehead crowned
With bay leaves, golden berries shining through them,
Promising Thebes relief. So, Creon, tell us
What news from the Delphic oracle?

CREON

(*His attitude to* OEDIPUS *is slightly ironic.*)
Good news. The worst diseases, if the right
Remedies are used, can be put right.

OEDIPUS

                                        Your words
Bring neither comfort nor despair
What did the oracle pronounce?

CREON

(*Looking round*)
> Must I speak to you before the whole of Thebes
> Or should we two go aside and talk together?

OEDIPUS

> Speak out before all. The grief I feel
> Is not just for myself but my whole people.

CREON

> Well then, I'll do so. Apollo says
> There is an evil thing we harbour
> Here in Thebes we must be purged of. Only
> If we do that will Thebes be saved.

OEDIPUS

> Purged? By what ritual? What can this evil be?

CREON

> Banish or execute a man
> Who has shed blood here: expiate
> Blood with blood – the victim's blood that brings
> The plague on Thebes.

OEDIPUS

> Who was the victim?

CREON

> Laius was King before you came to Thebes
> And saved us from the Sphinx – do you remember?

OEDIPUS

> I know that very well but never saw him.

CREON

Laius was murdered. Apollo now demands
That we take vengeance on the murderers
Without respect of whoever they may be.

OEDIPUS

Where could they be now? All trace
Of a crime so ancient must have vanished.

CREON

In this land, the god said. The guilty, if sought
Diligently, will not go uncaught.

OEDIPUS

Was it inside the palace? Or on the plain outside?
Or far abroad, that Laius met his end?

CREON

He was going to Delphi, so he said
When he set forth. He was not seen again.

OEDIPUS

Were there no witnesses? Did no one
Of those accompanying him return?

CREON

All but one died. He fled in terror
But swore to one thing as beyond question.

OEDIPUS

What was that thing? One clue might lead to all.

CREON

He said that not just one, but many
Robbers fell on Laius. A whole gang of them.

OEDIPUS

If they were more than one, they must have had
Accomplices in Thebes.

CREON

So it was said at the time. But Laius dead,
It was kept quiet in the turmoil that ensued.

OEDIPUS

Was regicide a crime to be ignored?

CREON

The riddling Sphinx kept that dark past obscured,
Fixing our mind on troubles nearer home.

OEDIPUS

(*Buoyantly*)

Well then I'll start the search afresh, and make dark
    light.
How right, though,
Of the oracle, and how right of you, my brother
To concern yourself with wrongs done to the dead.
My duty is to aid you now
In seeking vengeance – for Thebes' sake and Apollo's.
In doing so I act in my own interest too –
Those who killed Laius might seek to kill me also.
Get up, you suppliants with olive branches
Summon the Cadmeans to assemble here
So that before them all I can make known
That I intend – whatever be the consequences –

With the god's help, to restore Thebes to health.
If I don't succeed in this, we are lost, all of us.
(*Exeunt.*)

(*Enter* CHORUS *of* THEBAN ELDERS.)

CHORUS

O thrilling voice of Zeus
  come from Apollo's golden shrine
  with what intent towards us

   I tremble I faint I fail
   terror racks my soul

O Delian healer to whom my cries
from this abyss of despair arise

   What fate unknown until now
   or lost in the past and renewed
drawn from the revolving years
  will you send to us

O speak o tell me, immortal voice

    To Athena, daughter of Zeus,
  and her sister, Artemis,
    and Apollo of fiery arrows
   triple guardians of Thebes
    I call

If ever before in time past
you saved us from plague or defeat
   turn back to us now and save!

[35]

The plague invades
No knowledge saves
birth pangs of women
bring forth dead their children
life on life sped
to the land of the dead
like birds wing on wing
struck down from their flying
to the parched earth
by the marksman death

O Delian healer hear my prayer
star of my hope in my night of despair

grant that this god who without clash of sword on
    shield
fills with cries of our dying Thebes he makes his
    battlefield
        turn back in flight from us
            be made to yield

        driven by great gales favouring our side

to the far Thracian waters wave on wave
where none found haven ever but his grave

    O Zeus come with thy lightning to us
                                            save

        And come back Bacchus
Hair gold-bound and cheeks flame-red
        whom the Bacchantae worship and the Maenads
            led
        by his bright torch on high

Revelling again among us Bacchus and make death
The god whom gods and men most hate lie dead.

(*Re-enter* OEDIPUS, CHORUS, PRIESTS, *etc., as before.*)

OEDIPUS

You do well to pray.
And if you follow my instructions for saving you from
the plague all will yet be well with Thebes.
I say what I have to say now quite openly before you all
as one whose hands are completely clean and who
was not even in Thebes at the time of the violence. I
who address you Cadmeans became a Theban living
among you long after these events.
        If anyone here knows by whom Laius, son of
Labdacus, was killed, let him speak up now. And if the
murderer is here let him declare himself – for if he does
so at once he will have nothing worse to fear than being
sent abroad into exile unharmed. And if anyone among
you should know a foreigner among us who is the
murderer, let him denounce the guilty one and he will
receive due reward, together with my thanks.

((*A silence, after which* OEDIPUS *talks more rapidly.*)
Does no one answer?
If anyone of you here is now seeking to hide himself
    or his friend
or some foreigner from my enquiries
listen now to the penalties for collusion in the crime.
No one living in this land
may give shelter or hold converse with the guilty man:
nor join in prayers together with him:
nor make sacrifice or attend the lustral rites.
He is banned from every home of every one of you:
    for he is

[37]

the defilement denounced by the god.
Thebans, citizens,
I declare myself the ally of the god.
I lay this curse upon the hunted man,
wherever he may be – that evil
be visited on him as he did evil.

   This applies to me as to you all.
   If through my connivance he should be
   a dweller in my house, then let me suffer
   the same penalty as any other.
   I charge you all to carry out these orders
   for my sake and the god's and for this land's
   afflicted by the plague from heaven.
   Even had the oracle not spoken
   it still would be unseemly that the blood
   of Laius, your king, should not be avenged.
   And since I hold the powers that Laius held,
   being your king, married to your queen
      – Jocasta –
   and since Laius had no children and I have
   children by her who might have been the mother
   of his children, these things make ties
   between Laius and me as though he were
   Myself, I himself, husband of Jocasta.

CHORUS

Since you have put me on my oath to answer
I swear I did not murder Laius
Nor do I know who was his murderer.
Apollo knows. It would be best to ask him.

OEDIPUS

No one can force the god to speak.

CHORUS

If not the god, send for the priest, his servant
Teiresias, seer, the blind prophet,
Who in his dark can penetrate dark secrets.

OEDIPUS

This too I have thought of and have sent
Twice for Teiresias, who should be here by now.

CHORUS

Perhaps he will confirm the rumours.

OEDIPUS

What rumours? Tell me all you know.

CHORUS

That Laius was killed by many, not just one.

OEDIPUS

I have heard that too. But no witness has appeared.

(*Enter* TEIRESIAS *led by a* BOY.)

Teiresias, seer, prophet, you whose soul
Grasps at life's furthest roots – the love
That is spoken and that which has no name,
Heaven's highest mysteries and earth's darkest
   secrets.
Though blind, you have sight that sees into the cause
   of
The plague devouring Thebes, from which, great
   prophet,
You, our deliverer, alone can save us.
Phoebus, as earth's messengers may have told you,

[39]

Made answer to us by Creon, sent to Delphi,
That the sole cure for our affliction
Is to discover the murderers of Laius
And kill or banish them. Grant us your skills
Language of birds and necromancy
To save me, save Thebes, save this people.
You hold us in your hand, great prophet, you
Who know man's highest task is to help man.

TEIRESIAS

How dreadful to possess the knowledge
That does not benefit the one who knows it.
I knew this, then forgot it, now remember.
Would I had never come here.

OEDIPUS

What? You regret having come?

TEIRESIAS

Oedipus, let me go home. You'll bear
Better your burden till your life's end
and I mine, if you let me go now, at once –

OEDIPUS

Do not withhold your knowledge from us.
We suppliants implore you, on our knees.

TEIRESIAS

Because you do not know what you are asking –
But I'll not tell my grief – lest I tell yours.

OEDIPUS

You mean – you know the truth but will not say it?
That way you betray both us and Thebes.

[40]

TEIRESIAS

I have no wish to hurt you or myself.
Why have unnecessary knowledge?
You'll never drag the truth from me.

OEDIPUS

(*Losing his temper*)
Wretch, you'd try the patience of a stone.
Why do you temporize? Why don't you answer?
What can I do to make you speak?

TEIRESIAS

Whether I speak or remain silent
The future will reveal all just the same.

OEDIPUS

Since it is bound to do so, why not speak?

TEIRESIAS

I've said enough. Go on. Shout. Burst your lungs.

OEDIPUS

Yes, I'll go on. I'll follow your advice
And my own search, wherever they may lead.
You are the conspirator who plotted
The crime, and would yourself have done it,
Had you but the eyes.

TEIRESIAS

You dare say that? Let me warn you, King Oedipus.
Obey your own decree: and from this moment
Do not speak to the Thebans or to me:
You are the defilement that you seek.

[41]

OEDIPUS

You dare say that? And expect to go scot free?

TEIRESIAS

Free? I am free already in my truth.

OEDIPUS

Has someone taught you to be insolent?
You did not learn this, weaving spells.
Who put you up to it?

TEIRESIAS

You forced me to speak out against my will.

OEDIPUS

(*Dazed*)

Against your will? Say what you mean.

TEIRESIAS

Did not you understand, or do you wish
To tempt me to say more?

OEDIPUS

It seemed so dark. I did not grasp your meaning.

TEIRESIAS

You are the murderer of the man
Whose murderer you seek.

OEDIPUS

You will pay dearly for having said that.

TEIRESIAS

Shall I say more and make you angrier still?

[42]

OEDIPUS

Go on. All that you say is meaningless.

TEIRESIAS

Not knowing who you are, you live
In obscene intimacy with those
Who are your kin, and do not see
The miserable condition that is you.

OEDIPUS

You think you'll go from here unpunished?

TEIRESIAS

Yes, if there's any strength in truth.

OEDIPUS

For everyone but you. For you
There is no strength since you are blind
In ears, and mind, and eyes.

TEIRESIAS

Unhappy man to taunt me for those things
Everyone will soon be saying of you.

OEDIPUS

Unending night imprisons you within
The tomb which is your body, where you can harm
No one outside, who looks upon the sun.

TEIRESIAS

True, it is not I who'll cause your downfall.
Apollo has the eyes to see to that.

[43]

OEDIPUS

Is this your plotting or is it Creon's?

TEIRESIAS

No need of Creon. You yourself suffice.

OEDIPUS

See how my power and riches, statesmanship,
More skilled than any king's before me,
Draw to my greatness – which I never sought –
Power being thrust upon me – envy's
Searing edge, and that from Creon.
Him I most trusted, Creon, my wife's brother;
Creon who creeps up on me now
Seeking to overthrow me: for which purpose
He hires this swindler with eyes only
For his own gain, in everything else blind,
No nonsense now! Out with the truth!
Since when were you a seer? When the Sphinx
Wove her dark tapestry of song,
Were you the one who freed the people?
That riddle was not anyone's to read.
Who is the creature who has four legs, first,
Then two, then three: the answer – Man, who crawls
On all fours like a baby then stands on two,
Then with a staff in old age has three legs.
It was I, Oedipus, who solved the riddle
And killed the Sphinx and freed the people
With my own wits, untaught by any bird.
I you now seek to overthrow, so you may
Mutter in Creon's ear behind his throne.
I think the two of you will soon regret it.

CHORUS LEADER

Oedipus, Teiresias, both of you
Speak in anger words that do not help
Us carry out the god's command.

TEIRESIAS

Although you are the king, I share the privilege
To make reply, equal with yours.
Creon is not my master; Phoebus Apollo is.
I am not paid for services by Creon.
Since you taunt me with blindness, let me tell you –
Though you have sight, you cannot see
The truth of your own life: not whom you live with
Nor from what lineage you derive; nor how,
Unknowingly, you are the enemy
Of your own parents on earth, and in Hades below.
The double-twisted thong, your parents'
Rage conjoined, will one day drive you,
Precipitately, from this land
Unending darkness pouring
Through holes where were your eyes that see me now.
The valleys will re-echo with your shrieks
Reverberating through Cythaeron,
When you have learned the truth about your
    marriage –
That fatal port of setting forth so favoured.
Innumerable ills, today undreamed of,
Will thrust you down to your true height:
You and your whelpish mongrel brood.
Mock Creon, mock me, mock my message.
No one will end so unhappily as Oedipus.

OEDIPUS

Get out of here this instant! Leave me!

[45]

TEIRESIAS

I never would have come but that you asked me.

OEDIPUS

How could I tell that all you say is madness?
Had I known this, I never would have asked you.

TEIRESIAS

What you call mad makes good sense to your parents.

OEDIPUS

(*Dazed*)

My parents? Still talking of my parents?

TEIRESIAS

This day will see your birth and ending.

OEDIPUS

Riddles, always labyrinthine riddles.

TEIRESIAS

I thought that you were good at reading riddles.

OEDIPUS

Yes, mock me for that which is my greatness.

TEIRESIAS

Greatness? The masterstroke to your undoing!

OEDIPUS

All that I care for is that I saved Thebes.

TEIRESIAS

Saved Thebes! Well then I'll go. Boy, lead me.

[46]

OEDIPUS

Yes, let him take you. In your presence
My senses are bewildered and confused.
When you have gone, the day will clear again.

TEIRESIAS

One thing before I go. I'll answer
First what you asked.
Frown though you may, you cannot stop me.
He whom you seek, the murderer of Laius,
Is here: to all appearances
A stranger from abroad, but soon
He will be shown to have always been a Theban
And will not be the happier for the knowledge.
He'll soon be blind, who now can see – a beggar
Who now is rich, he'll find
His way out of the city with a stick
Tapping stone by stone the ground before him.
Father and brother to his children, son and husband
Of her who bore him, murderer
Of his own father. Now go inside
And ponder on what I have told you.
And when you find I am wrong will be the time
To say I have no gift for prophecy.

(TEIRESIAS *is led out by the* BOY.)

CHORUS

(*Speaking in several voices*)
Who is   where is   who is
that man
the man the sacred voice denounced
from the Delphic rock   the man
with blood-soaked hands who did

[47]

deeds too obscene for tongue to speak
time has come when he must run
on feet swifter than hoofs
of storm-scared steeds   for the son
of Zeus bounds after him
Apollo lightning-arrowed   bringing
the inexorable fates

Again again the message flashes
from snowy-peaked Parnassus
Make the chase now close in on
him who in the wilderness
through rocks and caves unhappy roams
like hunted bull flanks quivering
seeking to escape the doom
Thundered from earth's navel-stone.

CHORUS LEADER

Never though shall I agree
that the target of the chase
rightly could be Oedipus
Such thoughts daze me and confuse
Was it not our king who saved us
the incursion of the Sphinx
answered the riddle and did
noble service to the state?
That is what my heart tells me.

(*Enter* CREON.)

CREON

I am here because I am furious.
From all sides I hear that Oedipus has been making
   abominable

[48]

accusations against me.
If, amid our present disasters, he imagines
that he has suffered injury from me, I can only say
I would sooner not live out my allotted span of life
    and die at once
than hear such slanders coming from him.
Better be dead than pronounced
a traitor here before you all.

CHORUS

Do not take things in that spirit, Creon.
Oedipus is greatly troubled –
What he said he did not mean.

CREON

Did he say I bribed Teiresias?

CHORUS

Many things were said. I doubt he meant any of them.

CREON

When he was talking, did you judge him sane?

CHORUS

It's not for us to judge our leaders' sanity.
But here he comes himself. Here is King Oedipus.

(*Enter* OEDIPUS.)

OEDIPUS

You! How dare you have the impertinence
To come to this place where you have planned
The assassination of its king.
You, the shameless robber of my crown.

[49]

In the god's name tell me now, was it
My cowardice or my folly gave you courage
To plot against me? Did you take me for
A drooling idiot incapable
Of guarding myself against your schemes?
So that, without backers or supporters,
All on your own, you could drive me from my throne?

CREON

Listen to me, Oedipus, give my answer
To your accusations a fair hearing.
Then judge the matter on the arguments.

OEDIPUS

Cunning words, but I'm not wise in
Arguing along lines laid down by enemies.

CREON

You are not wise to think that obstinacy
And refusing to listen can replace reason.

OEDIPUS

You are not wise to think that treachery
Against a brother will go unpunished.

CREON

Certainly, if I thought that, I would be unwise.
If I have wronged you, tell me. How have I, Oedipus?

OEDIPUS

Did you not advise me to send for that quack?

CREON

Teiresias? I'd do the same again.

OEDIPUS

Unless he'd been egged on by you,
He'd never have accused me
Of being the murderer of Laius.

CREON

The murderer of Laius?
That's the first time I heard that said.

OEDIPUS

I'll never be found guilty of his blood.

(*Pause.*)

CREON

Oedipus, tell me this. Are you married to my sister?

OEDIPUS

That is a charge I would never deny.

CREON

And she and you have equal powers?
Ruling as king and queen?

OEDIPUS

Yes.

CREON

Do I not make a third, with you, having power
Equal with yours, the king's and the queen's?

OEDIPUS

That's why your treachery is so monstrous –
So false as friend and brother.

[51]

CREON

Not treachery, friend, be reasonable, as I am.
Ask yourself now – would any man of sense
Wish to be enthroned in the public gaze,
Confronted each day by new trials,
If he could exercise powers equalling a king's
Quietly, uncrowned, behind the scene?
I have no yearning to be king.
Without that name of king, I have the influence
To perform kingly deeds while men
Trust me and like me, greet me in the marketplace.
Now, those who lack access to you, ask me
To intercede for them with you, I being
Their only hope of getting near you.
Why exchange powers I have for those
I do not have? It would be mad.
But if you don't believe me, send to Delphi:
Ask the oracle if I lied.
If you find proof I plotted with Teiresias
Sentence me to death at once. You'll have two voices,
Yours and my own, for such a verdict.
Put me on public trial, but do not try me
In some dark corner where nothing need be proved.

CHORUS

He speaks like a subtle statesman
Defending his carefully thought out position.

OEDIPUS

(*To* CHORUS)

When the cunning plotter steps up stealthily
I must be swift in counter-action.
If I wait passively, he'll seize
His opportunity before I act.

[52]

CREON

Do you intend to throw me into exile?

OEDIPUS

Not banishment. I want your death
To show that envy is a monstrous crime.

CREON

You don't believe a word I've said?

OEDIPUS

Nothing you've said makes you sound credible.

CREON

Nothing you've said makes you sound sane.

OEDIPUS

Sane enough to guard my interests.

CREON

Justice requires that you guard mine as well.

OEDIPUS

I must guard my authority as king.

CREON

Not if you are a tyrant.

OEDIPUS

(To CHORUS)
Treachery! Rebellion! You've heard him, Thebans!

CREON

Thebes hears my voice equally with yours.

[53]

(*Enter* JOCASTA.)

JOCASTA
What is this noise? This brawling?
Why do you two brothers quarrel?
Aren't you ashamed to be bickering while the plague
Kills tens of thousands in Thebes – is this a time to air
Your private differences? Oedipus,
Go back into the palace, Creon,
Go home to your own house.

CREON
Jocasta, sister! Oedipus seeks my banishment or
    death.

OEDIPUS
Indeed I do, my queen, I found this man
Weaving spells and plotting to destroy me.

CREON
If that is true, may Zeus with all his thunder
Strike me down this instant. I deny it.

JOCASTA
Oedipus, you hear him? Then accept his solemn
    word.

CHORUS
Oedipus, think. Consent. Accept. Stop.
This quarrelling has gone too far already.

OEDIPUS
What favour are you asking of me?

CHORUS

Respect a counsellor who has never
Acted unwisely. Accept his words, his oath.

OEDIPUS

What you are asking is my banishment.

CHORUS

(*Speaking in several voices*)
No! No! O king! I swear
By Phoebus Apollo that is not true.
Let me be struck down on the instant
If I desire your banishment.
You saved Thebes from the Sphinx. I would be mad
Not to be grateful to you, always.
But see – I am worn out, desperate, overwrought
On account of Thebes – the plague,
It is more than I can bear – having to listen
To you two princes quarrelling.

OEDIPUS

Let him go then. I know that I am doomed.
Your words, not his, have made me change my mind.
Whatever he does or says is always
Poison, pernicious, hateful to me.

CREON

Sullen in yielding, angry in argument,
Natures like yours bring their own punishment.

OEDIPUS

Leave me in peace now and get out.

CREON

I'll go. I find you undiscerning.
These citizens will find me innocent.
(*To* CHORUS)
You who have seen him rage, take warning.

(*Exit* CREON.)

CHORUS

Queen Jocasta, why don't you go with the King into
    the palace?

JOCASTA

Before I go, I want to hear what happened.

CHORUS

On Creon's side, suspicion fed on hearsay.
On the King's, impatience and intemperate anger.

JOCASTA

(*To* OEDIPUS, *whom she takes aside*)
What reason do you have for your anger with Creon?

OEDIPUS

Because he has been plotting against me.

JOCASTA

How did the quarrel between you two begin?

OEDIPUS

He says I am guilty of the blood of Laius.

JOCASTA

Is that his own idea? Or does it come from some other
source?

OEDIPUS

He spreads it through that seer. He keeps his own lips
clean.

JOCASTA

O, Teiresias! Then consider yourself guiltless of any
crime! Oracles! Prophecies! I'll tell you now something
that will show what their science is worth. Once a
messenger came to Laius from the oracle at Delphi to
inform us that he was fated to die by the hand of his
son – his child and mine. It happens though that
Laius died at the hands of robbers – foreigners – at
some place where three roads meet.

OEDIPUS

(*As though he were seeing the place before his eyes*)
Where three roads meet?

JOCASTA

Moreover, in order to prevent there being any
possibility of the prophecy coming true, when our son
was only three days old, Laius had his ankles pinned
together, and him thrown – our only child – on to a
bare mountainside.

So how could Apollo make it come to pass that
that poor baby – its ankles shackled and cast out to
die – should murder his father as the prophecy
foretold? That's what their prophecies are worth!
Forget them all, Oedipus. And forget this wild goose
chase after the murderer. If Apollo wants to find out
who it is, he can do so for himself.

[57]

OEDIPUS

What scenes of horror
Rush through my brain, hearing you speak –
What did you say? What did you just tell me?
Where three roads meet? Laius was killed
Where three roads meet?

JOCASTA

That's what was said at the time. No one's ever
contradicted it.

OEDIPUS

Where? Where? What was the place called?

JOCASTA

Phosis, I think. Yes, Phosis. Roads do meet there; one
coming from Delphi, the other from Daulia.

OEDIPUS

How long ago did these events occur?

JOCASTA

Just before you became king.

OEDIPUS

Gods! Gods! What have you decreed for Oedipus?

JOCASTA

Why should these things disturb you?

OEDIPUS

Tell me this then. How tall was Laius? What age was he?

JOCASTA

About your height. A few silver hairs threaded among
black curls.
Yes, a bit like you are now.

OEDIPUS

Like me! Unhappy to be me. Have I not unwittingly
laid myself under some terrible curse?

JOCASTA

What are you talking about? You terrify me.

OEDIPUS

O O O O, that seer could see all right! Yet, to make
certain, tell me one thing more.

JOCASTA

See, I'm trembling – but I'll tell you all I know.

OEDIPUS

Did Laius go with just a few followers, or with a great
retinue, like a king?

JOCASTA

Five. There were just five. A herald in front of a
carriage. Only one. A driver. Two servants, and
Laius, my husband.

OEDIPUS

Yes. I see it all. Now. Passing before my eyes. And
who told you about it, Jocasta, my wife, my queen?

JOCASTA

The only survivor. There was no other. A servant.

[59]

OEDIPUS

A servant. A slave? Is he here now? In the palace?

JOCASTA

(*Distracted*)

What are you talking about? Oh. The servant. No he
isn't here. When he got back and was told that you
had become king, he implored me – went down on
his knees, clutching at my dress – to send him away –
anywhere – as a shepherd in the countryside – in the
fields – tending the flocks – anywhere, he said, except
the city. He begged me. Finally I let him go. He was a
worthy fellow. He could have done better for himself.

OEDIPUS

Send for him now – immediately.

JOCASTA

Well, that might be arranged. But why?

OEDIPUS

I may have been rash, too hasty in some things I said
to Creon. I must question the servant.

JOCASTA

I'll do as you ask. But as your wife I have the right to
know what is upsetting you.

OEDIPUS

Yes, I should keep nothing from you. Now gone so
far, you are my wife. We are together. Listen then!
    As you know, my father is Polybus of Corinth,
my mother is Merope, the Dorian. I was brought up
as the foremost citizen of Corinth. But one day

[60]

something happened which was disturbing, though
not in itself enough to justify the anger I felt. At a
banquet, one of the guests, who was drunk, yelled at
me that I was not really the son of Polybus. I managed
at the time to restrain myself, but next morning I
questioned my father and mother about it. They were
indignant at what the man had shouted. I was
reassured but doubt still lingered in my mind. So,
without my parents' knowledge, I went to the oracle
at Delphi. Phoebus Apollo didn't enlighten me as to
my origins, but to other questions gave horrifying
answers: that I should defile my mother's bed: raise a
brood of children abhorrent to mankind: lastly, that I
should kill my father.

After hearing this, I went as far as I possibly
could from Corinth, calculating by the stars some
region where it would be impossible for these
prophecies ever to come true.

On my way, I came to the place where three
roads meet, where you say King Laius met his death.
I'll tell you exactly what happened – A herald
approached me. Behind him, was a man seated in a
carriage drawn by two colts. The driver of the carriage
and the man inside it attempted to push me off the
path, out of their way.

Furious, I hit the driver. The other man, the
passenger, watched what I was doing, from where he
sat inside the carriage. Then, at the moment when the
carriage passed me standing there, he struck me on
the head with his double-thonged whip. Oh, he paid
dearly for this. With one blow from the staff I held in
my hand, I struck him from behind, and sent him
spinning down the mountainside to his death. Then I
disposed of the others also. Killed the lot.

[61]

But if this absolute stranger to me had any blood
ties with Laius, your husband, who is more miserable
than I?

Whom could heaven detest more?

A man whom no citizen of Thebes may receive into
his home: rather, indeed, who must be driven from it.

And this curse on me decreed by none other than
myself!

And you – his wife – wife of the man I murdered,
whom I married – this marriage – ours –

polluting the bed of the slain man.

Am I not a pariah? Loathsome? Utterly unclean?

Condemned by my own edict to banishment and
  in that exile

not able even to go back to my own parents

for fear I marry Merope, my mother, or slay my
  father, Polybus,

thus completing the fulfilment of the prophecy.

Would you not say that if there were someone

who stood outside, an onlooker of these events,
  he would

not agree they had been planned by some
  malicious power above,

intent upon my utter ruin?

O you all-witnessing heaven spare me

the final prophecy fulfilled

of marrying my mother, murdering my father

sweep me into the shadows from this world

before that final consummation.

CHORUS

O King, to us these things seem fearful too.

Yet hope remains still with that servant

Whom, the queen says, bore witness to the crime.

[62]

OEDIPUS

Yes all depends now on the herdsman.

JOCASTA

And when he has arrived, what of it?

OEDIPUS

Well, if his story fits with yours,
I shall be cleared of all suspicion.

JOCASTA

(*Wildly*)

What makes you certain of that?

OEDIPUS

You said that Laius was killed by many
Robbers, not one. So if the shepherd speaks
Of many murderers, that proves me innocent.

JOCASTA

I am sure that was his story, when he first got back to
Thebes. He can't change it now. The whole city heard
it. But even supposing he should alter it slightly, that
still won't make you be the man named in the
prophecy. Laius was quite definite that Apollo said he
would be killed by our son the only child of Laius and
me. But that poor baby can't possibly have killed him
since he himself died. So much for their prophecies!

OEDIPUS

What you say is surely true. But send for the
herdsman. I must enquire into everything.

[63]

JOCASTA

Let us now go back into the palace. You see how I do
all I can to please you.

(*Exeunt* OEDIPUS *and* JOCASTA.)

CHORUS
(*To be said in the manner of responses: psalm-like; liturgical*)

May fate keep me forever on the strict path of truth
and purity in word and deed, ordained by divine
laws:
Written in the empyrean, called into being by Zeus,
the father of Olympus
sublime above the race of mortal men, unageing and
not subject to death:
the god is mighty in them, nor do they grow old.

Insolence breeds the tyrant: gluttony surfeited on
wealth
and having attained the pinnacle of arrogance
he falls precipitately into the abyss.
And yet I pray the god not to forbid
competition that benefits the state.
Praise be to god, our heavenly preserver.

If a man in deed and word walks haughtily
not fearing justice, not revering
the gods, may ill doom down him
for pride insulting to the stars.
If he has gained power unjustly
not holding back from profane actions
but laying hands on what is sacred.

[64]

CHORUS LEADER

Where such things happen
What mortal being can be sure
he can ward off the arrows of the gods?
And how should I, the leader of the chorus
Take part in the sacred dance?
The centre of the world no longer holds.
The statues of the gods are overthrown.

(*Enter* JOCASTA *carrying a wreathed olive branch.*)

JOCASTA

Citizens of Thebes, I had this thought:
To visit the shrines of the gods, bringing
In my hands this olive branch
And gifts of incense. Oedipus
Has become so nervous, agitated,
Starting at nothings, most unlike a seasoned leader
Who measures bad news against precedents,
He rushes to conclusions drawn from messages.
Since all advice I give him goes unheeded
I have come to you, Apollo, to your shrine,
It being the nearest. I pray to you
To accept these offerings, O and save us
From the spreading nightmare. We are terrified
Like a crew whose helmsman is distraught.

(*Enter* MESSENGER.)

MESSENGER

Sirs, can you direct me to the house of King Oedipus?
Or, better still, to the King himself?

[65]

CHORUS

This is the house, and he himself is inside. This lady,
Queen Jocasta, is mother of his children.

MESSENGER

And may this blessed lady stay blessed, since she's his
wife and mother of his children.

JOCASTA

And may so gracious greeting meet as gracious
thanks. What is your message then?

MESSENGER

Well, as you might say, bad news which is good
news, good news which is bad news. Paradoxical.

JOCASTA

Wherein lies the paradox?

MESSENGER

Well, on the one hand it's good – he'll be crowned
King of Isthmia – on the other hand it's bad. His
father is dead.

JOCASTA

What's that you say? His father, the aged Polybus, is
dead?

MESSENGER

Didn't I tell you he deceased?

JOCASTA

(*To a* SERVANT)

Go quickly. Tell your master at once to come here!
Prophecies! Oracles! See where they stand now! The

father of Oedipus dead! The man Oedipus went in
fear of seeing because the oracle prophesied he would
murder him.

(*Enter* OEDIPUS.)

Just listen to what this good fellow has to tell you,
Oedipus, and then let me hear what you have to say
about oracles.

OEDIPUS

What news does he bring?

JOCASTA

He is from Corinth, come to tell you that your father
Polybus is dead.

OEDIPUS

(*To* MESSENGER)

Can this be true? Let me hear it from your own
mouth.

MESSENGER

It is my job to state plain truths plainly, Polybus is
dead.

OEDIPUS

Was he murdered? Or did he die a natural death?

MESSENGER

Oh, he was getting on in years. At that time of life
drop a feather in the scale, and they're across the
River Styx.

[67]

OEDIPUS

That's true, alas! Jocasta, why should I look to
Apollo's shrine, or eagles screaming prophecies in
the sky above our heads? One that foretold that I
should kill my father? For he is dead and wandering
under earth, and I alive, who never raised spear at
him – unless, indeed, he died through missing me so
that my absence made me his murderer. No. Polybus
has taken down to Hades, together with him, those
lying oracles. Now they are vanished. All they said
was false.

JOCASTA

Did not I say that to you long ago?

OEDIPUS

And you were right. My fears misled me.

JOCASTA

From now on, Oedipus, fear nothing.

OEDIPUS

I think that I still fear my mother's bed.

JOCASTA

Why should man, who is mortal, and his whole fate
subject to chance, of which he can foresee nothing at
all, fear anything? It is best to live unheeding day to
day. Have no fear of marrying Merope – many a man
has made love to his mother in fantasizing dreams.
Those fare best who learn to ignore such fleshly
phantoms.

[68]

OEDIPUS

These words of yours would have more force if my
mother were dead, but she's still living.

JOCASTA

(*With a shade of contempt*)
Your father's dead. Let that reassure you.

OEDIPUS

My mother is living still. That's what I fear.

MESSENGER

Excuse my interrupting, sir. But who's this woman
whom you say you fear?

OEDIPUS

Merope, wife of Polybus, who has died.

MESSENGER

And what would make you afraid then of Queen
Merope?

OEDIPUS

A message from the Delphic oracle.

MESSENGER

Would it be lawful to ask what the message is?

OEDIPUS

The oracle prophesied that I was doomed to marry my
mother and kill my father, that is why I forsook my
dear parents in Corinth; sweet though it was to look
into their eyes.

[69]

MESSENGER

Was that why you fled from Corinth?

OEDIPUS

Those were my reasons.

MESSENGER

You are afraid of the prophecy about your parents?

OEDIPUS

That is the fear I have lived with all these years.

MESSENGER

Well, all those years you had nothing to be afraid of.

OEDIPUS

What do you mean?

MESSENGER

What I mean is – they weren't your parents.

OEDIPUS

How can that be? I was their son.

MESSENGER

Merope was not your mother.
Polybus was not your father.

OEDIPUS

How? How?

MESSENGER

No more your father than I. In fact, less, in a manner
of speaking.

[70]

OEDIPUS

How could my father, who was King, be the equal of
you, a slave?

MESSENGER

Because he received you as a gift from my hands.

OEDIPUS

Polybus loved me as a son.

MESSENGER

That's simple. Because he had no son of his own.
Merope and Polybus were childless.

OEDIPUS

You – did you buy me at a slave market?
How? Where?

MESSENGER

Abandoned among Cythaeron's hills.

OEDIPUS

And how did you happen to be there, my man?

MESSENGER

(*Sullenly*)

I was a mountain shepherd tending the flocks.

OEDIPUS

A shepherd, you say? A tramp? A vagrant?

MESSENGER

To you a shepherd and your saviour.

[71]

OEDIPUS

In what condition was I when you found me?

MESSENGER

The scars upon your ankles will tell that.

OEDIPUS

Why remind me of that long-ignored blemish?

MESSENGER

I found you with your ankles pinned together.

OEDIPUS

Was it my father or my mother pinned them?

MESSENGER

He who gave you to me can answer that.

OEDIPUS

Another man! You said it was you who found me.

MESSENGER

Another shepherd gave you to me first.

OEDIPUS

Who? Who? Where from? Can you remember?

MESSENGER

He said it was the house of Laius.

OEDIPUS

From the house of Laius? From the King?

MESSENGER

He was a herdsman in his service.

OEDIPUS

Is this herdsman living still, so I may see him?

MESSENGER

(*Turning to* CHORUS)
 You country folks are the ones to answer that.

OEDIPUS

Does any of you know the herdsman's whereabouts?
The hour draws close when all will be made clear.

CHORUS

He means the same man as the queen sent for
The slave who fled when you were made the King.

OEDIPUS

(*To* JOCASTA)
 Was the servant whom you sent for the same man?

JOCASTA

What does it matter who he was?
Ignore it, Oedipus.

OEDIPUS

I have to know the truth about my birth.

JOCASTA

Oedipus, if you care for me or for yourself –
The anguish that I suffer – you'll stop now.
Stop. Give up this chase.

[73]

OEDIPUS

Supposing I should find myself to be
Born of slave stock like this man's,
That doesn't make you base-born too.

JOCASTA

For your own sake listen to me. Stop. Don't go on!

OEDIPUS

Yes, to the end. I must go on. I have to know.

JOCASTA

Fool! Damned! Never discover who you are!

OEDIPUS

Go – fetch the slave, the herdsman. Let her stay
Proud of her high birth, and howl her fill.
She fears she's married to slave blood.

JOCASTA

Blind! Blind! That's the last word you'll ever hear from
    me.
Blind! Blind! Blind!

(*She rushes out.*)

CHORUS

Why has Jocasta rushed out, Oedipus,
Distraught with passionate weeping? I fear
Some terrible breakdown will follow.

OEDIPUS

Break what may! Let the world break! I have to know
My origins, base-born though I may be.

[74]

With more even than most women's vanity
She fears she's married to a slave's son. I'm content
To see myself a child of fortune – sometimes up
Sometimes down. I accept that.
I must be true to what I am, whatever
Or whoever that may prove to be.

CHORUS
(*One voice only: a lyrical intermezzo*)
If I still have the gift of prophecy,
O hills and valleys of lovely Cythaeron,
I swear that by tomorrow at full moon
Oedipus will recognize in you
Mother and nurse and native land he grew in.
So these, because they pleased our King, we sing
And to Apollo may they too prove pleasing.

Who was it fathered you, and who conceived you,
Child, among these hills, by moon or noon?
Was it to Pan some wandering nymph bore you
While he roamed the mountainside? Or may it have
    been
Some bride Apollo favoured? Or even
Bacchus, god of the Bacchantae, received you
A gift from a nymph on Helicon,
One of those he most delights to play with?

(*Enter* HERDSMAN.)

OEDIPUS
Is this the herdsman?

MESSENGER
If it's not him it's his spitting image.

[75]

OEDIPUS

Old fellow, look me straight in the eyes.
Answer my question.
You were in the service of Laius. Is that true?

HERDSMAN

Reared in his palace as a slave. Not bought.

OEDIPUS

What was your position in the palace?

HERDSMAN

(*Evasive*)
Most of my life, I have tended flocks.

OEDIPUS

In what region did you tend them?

HERDSMAN

Cythaeron, all that part round there.

OEDIPUS

(*Pointing to* MESSENGER)
Do you remember ever having seen that man?

HERDSMAN

What man? Him there? Doing what?

OEDIPUS

This man, fool. Have you ever seen him before?

HERDSMAN

Not so I can be certain I remember.

[76]

MESSENGER

Perhaps I can jog his memory, sir.

(*Addressing* HERDSMAN)

Don't you tell me you don't remember as well as I do
how the two of us tended our flocks near Cythaeron,
you with your two, I, your mate, with my one – all of
three years, from spring to winter, when I drove my
flock to my fold and you drove your flock to the fold
of Laius. Was this so or wasn't it so?

HERDSMAN

I wasn't saying it wasn't so, was I?

MESSENGER

(*Sarcastic*)

I suppose you'll be saying next you forget giving me a
baby boy and asking me to bring him up –

HERDSMAN

That's none of my business now nor none of yours.

MESSENGER

Well just look at him standing there. He's that child.

HERDSMAN

(*Lunging at* MESSENGER)

Shut your trap, won't you?

OEDIPUS

Leave him alone. You're more at fault than he is.

HERDSMAN

What have I done wrong, your reverence?

[77]

OEDIPUS

Not answering him about the child.

HERDSMAN

He doesn't know where what he asks will lead.

OEDIPUS

Answer, or I'll find means to make you.

HERDSMAN

You wouldn't hurt an old man who never harmed
you.

OEDIPUS

Seize him. Pinion him. Don't let him go.

(GUARDS *seize* HERDSMAN.)

HERDSMAN

What do you want to know you don't know?

OEDIPUS

Did you give this man that child?

HERDSMAN

I wish I'd died the day I did so.

OEDIPUS

You'll die now if you don't tell all.

HERDSMAN

And if I tell, then I'll be worse than dead.

[78]

OEDIPUS

It seems he's set on being obstinate.

HERDSMAN

I've told you I gave him the child.

OEDIPUS

Whom did you get the child from?

HERDSMAN

Don't ask to know more, master, don't ask more.

OEDIPUS

You're dead unless you answer – and at once.

HERDSMAN

The child was from the house of Laius.

OEDIPUS

Was it a slave – a base-born child – a slave – or his
own blood?

HERDSMAN

The truth you force out chokes my throat.

OEDIPUS

And bursts my heart. Go on, for I must know.

HERDSMAN

Since you must know – they said it was his child.
Your lady, the Queen's the one who knows – ask her.

OEDIPUS

The Queen? She gave the child to you?

[79]

HERDSMAN
She did, O son of Laius, royal Oedipus.

OEDIPUS
Why?

HERDSMAN
To do away with it.

OEDIPUS
Why? Why? Why?

HERDSMAN
To stop the prophecy from coming true.

OEDIPUS
What prophecy?

HERDSMAN
Apollo said the son would kill his father.

OEDIPUS
Why did you give him to this old man then?
Why did you let the child live?

HERDSMAN
For pity, and for thinking he would take him
To that far land from which he came himself.
But I see now I saved him for that fate
To which you, if you are that man, were born.

OEDIPUS
All happened, all came true, it is the end.
Cursed in my birth, cursed in my marriage, cursed

[80]

In that fate of murdering my father!
Light, let me look no more upon the world.

(*Exit* OEDIPUS.)

CHORUS

O human generations, I consider
Life but a shadow. Where is the man
Ever attained more than the semblance
Of happiness but it quickly vanished?
Oedipus, I count your life the example
Proving we can call no human blessed.

With skill incomparable he threw the spear;
He gained the prize of an unchallenged fame;
He killed the crooked-taloned maiden
Whose singing made the midday darken;
He was our tower that rose up against death
And from that day we called him King of Thebes.

But now whose history is more grievous
Plagued with the loss of all that greatness his?
Whose fortunes ever met with such reverse?
I pity Oedipus for whom that soft flesh couch
That bore him, also proved his nuptial couch,
Oh how can soil in which your father sowed
Have secretly endured your seed so long?

Time, all-revealing, finally tracked you down,
Condemned the monstrous marriage which begot
Your children upon her, your own begetter.
O son of Laius, would my eyes had never seen you.
I weep like one with lips formed for lament.
Until today it was you who gave me light;
Today your darkness covers up my eyes.

[81]

(*Enter* SECOND MESSENGER.)

SECOND MESSENGER

Jocasta, the Queen, is dead.

CHORUS

How did she die?

SECOND MESSENGER

By her own hand. Having left here
And gone into the palace, she rushed on
To where there was her bridal bed. She bolted fast
The bedroom's massive doors, then threw herself
On the great bed and cried, again, again,
The name of 'Laius', the King, her husband
Long since a corpse, killed by that son,
Oedipus, the father of her children.
How she bewailed that marriage and its brood!
Then with a great cry Oedipus ran through
The palace, crying out 'Jocasta', 'Wife!'
Till guided by some god to where she lay
He hurled himself against the double doors,
Wrenching them from their hinges. There he saw
Jocasta's body hanging from the roof-beam
By the neck, in a noose of twisted cords.
He cut the body down, and where it lay
Stretched on the floor, he tore away the brooches
Fastening her dress, and lifting them above him
Plunged the pinned clasps down on his eyes.

(*Enter* OEDIPUS, *the sockets of his eyes bleeding, the clasps of the brooches still held in his hands.*)

[82]

OEDIPUS

From now on, you'll see only night.

CHORUS

Most terrible of sights I ever witnessed!
Unhappy man, what madness overcame you?
Who is that supernatural enemy
At one bound tore you down?
I dare not look upon you; dare not ask,
Though there is much that I should look upon,
Much ask.

OEDIPUS

Whither am I borne upon my agony?
Where does my voice reach? Whom? How far
Into the dark my fate has taken me.

CHORUS

Into the uttermost realms of horror.

OEDIPUS

Dreadful the blackness that envelops me
Annihilating all, resistless –
Such end to setting forth so fair.
I feel the clasps that pierced my eyeballs
Penetrate to my soul with memories.

CHORUS

Pain of the flesh redoubled by the mind.

OEDIPUS

Dear friend, I still can feel, though cannot see
Your kindly presence there for the blind man.

CHORUS

Beyond all bounds as were your acts, what power
Brought you to that extreme of folly
The plucking out of your own eyes?

OEDIPUS

Apollo! Apollo! Apollo!
Brought on me all my sufferings.
But I myself with my own hands
Tore out my eyes.
Why should I have eyes when nothing
That they could see would bring delight?

CHORUS

Indeed, that is true.

OEDIPUS

My curse upon that man, whoever it was,
Who found the child cast on the barren hillside
And freed my ankles from the cruel fetters
And gave me back, when almost dead, to life!
Had I died then, I would not be this burden
To you, my friends, that I am now.

CHORUS

Better indeed if you had never lived.

OEDIPUS

Nor would I then have killed my father
Nor have been pointed at – the husband
Of her who bore me,
Son of a mother by myself defiled:
Usurper in the marriage bed – my father's,

Who gave me my own being.
What fate could be more miserable
Than to be Oedipus?

CHORUS

But better to be dead than blind.

OEDIPUS

Mock me no more with your clever knowingness –
Had I still eyes, how should I,
When I descend into the world below,
Look on my father and my mother –
Laius and Jocasta, against whom
My sins were such no strangling could atone for?
Do you suppose the sight of children, born
As mine were, could replenish
The gaze that rested on them? Or
The vision of this city with towered walls,
Groves sacred with the statues of the gods? For I,
Who was the foremost of the Thebans,
Myself pronounced the edict that the unclean,
Him whom the gods had shown to be unholy,
Must be thrust out and see these things no more.
O you three roads, coppice and sacred glen,
Narrow defile where three roads meet,
That drank my father's blood poured from my hands;
Do you remember my violence among you
And, after, when I came to Thebes, worse deeds
That I went on to do?
O marriage rites, my father's and my mother's,
That gave me birth and then bore children to me.
Their child – and made a kinship brothel,
Incestuous stew of father, mother,
Brothers, sisters – bestial, foulest stench –

[85]

Most shameful of all things men do
That dare not name their names. Friends,
Help me, for the god's sake hide me
Somewhere far from this land. Kill me, throw me
Into the soundless ocean depths, oblivion,
Where you shall never see me more.

(*Enter* CREON.)

CHORUS

Here is Creon come to restore order to the state.
Creon will take over now.

OEDIPUS

Creon – what shall I say to him? Creon, whose death I
sought.

CREON

Oedipus, I have not come here to crow over you in
your misfortune nor to reproach you for past errors.

(*To* CHORUS)

But as for you, even if you have no respect for your
fellow citizens, you should at least show some to our
god, the sun, who nourishes all life. Spare Apollo the
sight of such abomination – a scandal to the pure
earth and the sanctifying rain and the clean light. Get
this unseemly spectacle out of here into the decent
covering of darkness indoors where it is proper for his
kinsmen to conceal his hideous wounds.

OEDIPUS

Since you who are raised so high have stooped to visit
me who am cast down so low, may I beg of you a favour?

[86]

CREON

Well, if you insist.

OEDIPUS

Purge this land of my presence.

CREON

That would certainly be in accordance with my own feelings about the matter, but I must first send to Delphi.

OEDIPUS

Will you trouble the oracle about someone so
    insignificant as Oedipus?

CREON

Yes, no matter is too small for the god's attention.
Even you should know that by now. I shall send to
    the oracle.

OEDIPUS

That's why I beg a favour of you. Give my wife burial the same as you would give your wife. As for my children, the boys, Eteocles and Polyneices, can look after themselves. But my poor girls – Antigone and Ismene – those two children who shared every meal with me at the same table – let me touch them with my hands.

(ANTIGONE *and* ISMENE *are brought in.*)

Can these be my loved daughters I hear weeping?

[87]

CREON

I knew your love for them and had them brought
  here.

OEDIPUS

May heaven reward you more than it has me.
My daughters, where are you?
Come here and let me touch you with my hands
The hands of him whose mother was your mother
The hands of him who tore out his own eyes.
Blind when he had them, seeing nothing,
In ignorance he became your father
By her of whom he himself was born.
If I had those eyes, they'd weep
Thinking of the life men will make yours.
To what parties will you go, what festivals
From which you'll not come back in tears!
And when the day arrives that you should marry
Where is the husband who will face such scoffing –
'Sisters of their father by their mother' –
I can hear the taunts already at the banquet.
Who would attend such weddings, were their youths
To be the bridegrooms of such brides?
You will be spinsters, barren, withered.
O Creon, brother of Jocasta, you
Their sole relation left to them –
Care for Antigone and Ismene
Save them from being unloved wanderers
Sunk to the abyss that is their father's.
Pity these orphans. No one but you
Can help. O be magnanimous, Creon. Lift your hand
And touch me as a sign that you will help them.

(CREON *raises his hand and quickly touches* OEDIPUS.)

Dear children, though too young to understand
Make this your prayer, to accept what life will bring
    you.
And pray you may be happier than your father.

CREON
You have said your fill. You are no longer King.
Now go into the house.

OEDIPUS
On what conditions?

CREON
Conditions? Well . . . State your needs and I will grant
    them.

OEDIPUS
Stone me. Kill me. Drive me out of Thebes.

CREON
Only Apollo can decide that.

(OEDIPUS *starts to go. Stumbles. Moves towards the* CHORUS *so
they may assist him. They draw away in terror of him.*)

OEDIPUS
Do not fear to touch me, fellow citizens.
I have taken on myself the plague
For all. And Thebes is saved.

(*One of the* CHORUS *gives him a staff, and assists him offstage.*)

[89]

CHORUS

Citizens of Thebes,
Here is Oedipus, who solved the riddle
And was most famous.
Who of you, gazing at him, was not envious?
Behold him now, wrecked by the stormiest seas.
Know then, we should call no man happy
Till he has passed that frontier where all pain ceases.

OEDIPUS AT COLONOS

Scene: Colonos, near Athens. A sacred grove, distant view of the
Acropolis, statue of the hero and founder of the place, the knight,
Colonos.
Enter OEDIPUS and ANTIGONE.

OEDIPUS

Where are we now, Antigone, my daughter?
What region? Near what city? Will those who live
    there
Provide for the blind wanderer?
Little I need, indeed less than that little,
Being schooled in patience by adversity,
Our dear companionship over long years
And some innate nobility of mind.
My daughter, if you see a place
Where I can rest, stop there
While you look round and find out where we are.

ANTIGONE

Far off, I see towered walls that guard a city,
Near where we stand, a sacred grove
With laurel, myrtle, vine. Nightingales
Pour forth their throbbing song from hidden depths.
Sit on this unhewn stone, dear father.
You have walked too far today already.

(Pause.)

OEDIPUS

Now can you tell me where this place is?

[93]

ANTIGONE

Near Athens. I do not know its name.

OEDIPUS

Yes. As we came here, everyone said Athens.

ANTIGONE

I see a stranger approaching. Ask him.

(*Enter* STRANGER.)

OEDIPUS

Sir, knowing from my daughter you are near
– she who is eyes to me who have no eyes –
May I ask where . . .

STRANGER

Before you ask me anything,
Get off that rock. It's unlawful
To be on holy ground here.

OEDIPUS

Sacred to what god?

STRANGER

These are the forbidden precincts of
The all-dreaded goddesses, guardians of Athens,
Daughters of earth and darkness.

OEDIPUS

How should I name them in my prayers?

STRANGER

The Eumenides, the people call them.

[94]

OEDIPUS

(*Kneeling*)

I'll kneel upon this earth and tell them
I am their suppliant come to die here
Never till death to leave their holy precincts.

STRANGER

Live here – a blind old wanderer – what do you
    mean?

OEDIPUS

The omens show this is my journey's end.

STRANGER

Stay here, while I run to ask
The guardians for instructions what to do with you.

OEDIPUS

Before you go, answer my question:
What is this place?

STRANGER

All here is sacred: sailor-dreaded Poseidon
Girds the coast round with tides.
Inland there burns the central flame
Of the fire-carrier Prometheus.
That place you desecrate by being there
Is the Brazen Threshold, gate of Athens.
The great equestrian statue that you see
Is of Colonos, lord and ancestor
Of these people who bear his name.

OEDIPUS

Do the people of Colonos have a king?

[95]

STRANGER

Theseus, King of Athens, is their ruler.

OEDIPUS

Could someone take a message to King Theseus?

STRANGER

What right have you, an old man, blind, a beggar
To send a message to King Theseus?

OEDIPUS

To grant my small request would bring him gain.

STRANGER

What benefit from the blind man?

OEDIPUS

Open his eyes.

STRANGER

Listen to me, friend, I would not have you
Come to harm. There is something noble
About your features, though marred by ill-fortune.
Wait here while I consult the village elders.
They will decide your future.

(*Exit* STRANGER.)

OEDIPUS

Is he gone? Are we alone, Antigone?

ANTIGONE

Yes, father, alone. Say what you please.

OEDIPUS

(*Kneeling*)

O queens of air and darkness, awesome powers,
First sacred spirits I have encountered
Here in Colonos, I kneel before you
Praying you incline your kindliest aspect
On me, not for my own sake only, but Apollo's –
For he, when he pronounced my fate, promised
That after many years of wandering
I should reach your shrine and that it would become
A haven for me, and would also bring
Benefit to my hosts, and ruin
To their enemies, mine also, those
Who drove me out of Thebes. He prophesied,
Moreover, at my end, conspicuous signs,
Earthquake and thunder, lightning,
From the hand of Zeus. Receive me then,
Kind daughters of primeval darkness
Into your grace, this wraith of Oedipus.

ANTIGONE

Hush father. Here come the village elders,
Doubtless in search of you.

OEDIPUS

It would be wise to know what they plan for me.
Hide me, where I can overhear them.

(ANTIGONE *hides him. Enter* CHORUS OF ELDERS.)

CHORUS

(*Several voices*)

Which way did he run?
Where has he gone?

[97]

Insolent vagabond!
Search every bush and hedge!
A stranger a foreigner,
Not from Athens, not from Colonos.
Trudging, intruding
Into the untrodden grove
Where the sacred vestals stand
Those we pious citizens dare not raise our eyes to look
     upon.

OEDIPUS

(*Coming out of hiding place*)
The blind have ears for seeing
The whereabouts of those that speak.
I am the man you seek.

CHORUS

(*They look at him then turn away.*)
O O O horrible
Too terrible to see or hear!

OEDIPUS

Friends, do not look upon me as an outlaw.

CHORUS

The gods defend us
Who can this blind old ruined wanderer be?

OEDIPUS

One in his life not so entirely fortunate
As to excite your envy –
Else, to walk, I would not need to lean on
The strength of this frail girl
Nor, to see, need her eyes.

[98]

CHORUS

(*Several voices*)
> Were you born blind?
> More likely became so through evil ways.
> A long long life of many ill-spent days.
> If you follow my advice
> It will spare you still worse trouble
> Move away from where you are
> For the ground is sacred there.
> Move this way. Stop. Not so far.
> Don't enter the sacred glade
> Where the fresh spring water mingles
> With honeyed drink offerings.
> If you wish to speak with us
> Move on to that further ledge of rock.

OEDIPUS

(*To* ANTIGONE)
> How shall I answer them, Antigone?

ANTIGONE
> Do as they ask. You have no choice – Take my hand,
> father.

OEDIPUS
> Here is my hand.

CHORUS
> Move on further – further –

ANTIGONE

(*Taking his hand and leading him*)
> Follow me, father, through your night
> Where I lead you with my sight.

[99]

OEDIPUS
Take me to the chosen spot
Where I can talk with them.

CHORUS
Stay where you are now. On that ledge of rock.

OEDIPUS
Will you promise sanctuary for me at this place?

CHORUS
We promise.
No one can move you from where you are standing
    now.

(OEDIPUS *has been placed there by* ANTIGONE.)

Stay where you are. Don't move.
Answer our questions.
Where do you come from?
Under what name do you journey?
In what city were you born?

OEDIPUS
The privilege of sanctuary is silence.

CHORUS
We have to know. Tell us who you are.

OEDIPUS
A name not to be named. Too terrible to tell.

CHORUS
Tell us! Tell us!
What is your family? Your home town?
Who is your king?

OEDIPUS
(*To* ANTIGONE)
What will become of me? My daughter,
What must I tell them?

ANTIGONE
Nothing but the truth, you have no choice.

OEDIPUS
(*Almost whispering*)
The house of Labdacus . . . The son of Laius . . .

CHORUS
(*Turning away in horror*)
A–a–a–ah!

OEDIPUS
I am Oedipus of the royal house of Thebes.

CHORUS
A–a–a–ah!

OEDIPUS
Do not turn your backs upon the exile
To whom you granted sanctuary.

CHORUS
(*They turn round, the better to shout at him.*)
Out with you! Out of here! Out of Colonos!

[101]

OEDIPUS

You promised sanctuary for me on this rock.

CHORUS

Promises made in ignorance don't count.
We did not know your name and history then.
Don't bring the plague that marks you upon us.
Out with you! Out of Colonos!

ANTIGONE

Respected, pious, virtuous folk of Colonos,
Who harden your hearts against my father
On account of deeds he did in ignorance,
Take pity at least on me his daughter,
Who ask it not for my sake but for his.
You, who have eyes that can look back in mine,
As I have eyes that can look back in yours,
Look on me now
As though I were your child, your daughter who,
If she were unhappy you would pity.
To us, my father and I, you are gods
Upon whose charity we depend.
You are our sole hope, so have mercy on us
I beg you by all that you hold dear –
Whether it be wife, child, money or a god.

CHORUS

Daughter of Oedipus, understand
We pity both of you in your misfortune
Only we fear to offend the gods.

OEDIPUS

(*Outburst*)

> Is this Athens? Athens? – What remains of that high
>   name
> For justice, fairness? Is this
> Athens: in the eye of heaven
> Pre-eminent among cities, famed
> For welcoming and nurturing the exile
> Seeking refuge from tyranny?
> Where do I find here that great heart of greatness –
> I, whom even now you hurried
> From the bare rock you promised me as sanctuary?
> So . . . would you drive me from Colonos?
> And all for fear of my name – Oedipus –
> My name only – not surely for my deeds
> Done unwittingly by one who was
> Their passive sufferer enacted on
> – Not their deliberate doer? You know the story
> – My father – mother – incest – murder –
> And, knowing it, when all is known
> How should you account me evil – a man who killed
> Justifiably, in self-defence, his assailant,
> Not knowing who he was? Those that did know
> They were the ones who sought my ruin.
> But you, since you honour the gods, you should
>   protect
> The exile, the god-fearing man
> Distinct in his affliction, and thus sacred.
> Do not defile the sacred name of Athens
> By driving out the one you promised sanctuary,
> But keep your serious pledge and succour me
> Even to my last day. Do not scorn
> This face that fate has ravaged. I am a man
> Sacrosanct through suffering, bringing

[103]

Benefits to your people I shall reveal
To your ruler, King Theseus, when he comes.

CHORUS

Oedipus, your words have shaken us.
As to your future, that will be determined
By our ruler, Theseus, King of Athens.

OEDIPUS

Where is King Theseus?

CHORUS

We have sent a messenger to bring him.

OEDIPUS

Why should he care to see one so afflicted?

CHORUS

To care, he only has to hear your name
Ringing throughout the world with stories of you.
When he knows you are here, he will want to see
    Oedipus.

OEDIPUS

Seeing me will bring him blessings
And on me too. The good reward the good.

(ISMENE *is seen approaching*.)

ANTIGONE

Oh, father, father, can I believe my eyes?

OEDIPUS

What is it, Antigone?

[104]

ANTIGONE

Far off, I see a woman approaching.
She is riding a pony. She's wearing her straw hat
From Thessaly, to keep off the sun's rays.
Can it be she? Am I dreaming?
No it isn't. Yes it is. I'm certain now –
Now she can see me.
        She's smiling at us
Yes. It is Ismene.

OEDIPUS

What? Where?

ANTIGONE

Ismene! Your daughter, my sister!
Soon you'll know her by her voice.

(ISMENE *enters.*)

ISMENE

Father! Sister! Loving names!
How I have been longing for you both.
I can hardly see you through my tears.

OEDIPUS

Can it be true that you are here?

ISMENE

Father, poor unhappy father!

OEDIPUS

Unhappy? Why I have my daughters with me.

ISMENE

It has been such a long long journey.

OEDIPUS

Touch me, my child.

ISMENE

Here is a hand for each of you.

OEDIPUS

Ah, children, children!

ISMENE

Alas, for all three of us!

OEDIPUS

Ismene, what brings you here?

ISMENE

To see you, father.

OEDIPUS

Just to see me?

ISMENE

Yes and to bring you news.

OEDIPUS

News! That can only be of your two brothers,
My sons. Where are they?

ISMENE

For them, as well as us, these are dark hours.

OEDIPUS

True models of effete Egyptians
For there, in Egypt, the men
Sit at home weaving, while their women
Work in the fields to earn their keep.
So these brothers stay home while you, the sisters,
Carry burdens for your father.
You, Antigone, from childhood have been
Guide to my wandering through parched deserts,
Rain-soaked valleys, howling forests,
Barefoot and hungry, parched and drenched,
The love between us our sole home,
Returned to with each moment; and you
Ismene, from far off, have kept watch
Warning of dangers behind or ahead,
Telling of the oracles, their prophecies.
Well, well, what news of your two brothers?

ISMENE

All I can tell is of their unhappiness.
Father, do not turn away, but listen!
At first, when you were exiled from Thebes, they
    wished
To give the throne to Creon, and thus spare
The city the curse cast upon our line.
But then, moved by some god, or their own sinful
    natures,
Each was seized with mad ambition to be king.
Eteocles, the younger, always the rash one,
Seized the throne from his brother Polyneices
Who has fled to mountain-surrounded Argos.
There, men say, he has formed a league of allies
With seven leaders who plan to fall on Thebes
And make him king backed by those foreign forces.

[107]

That is the terrible truth, father.
It is hard to see how the gods will spare us.

OEDIPUS

In spite of which you have faith I will be saved.

ISMENE

Yes, father. All the oracles say so.

OEDIPUS

What do they foretell?

ISMENE

They say the Thebans want you back
Alive or dead, for reasons of their own.

OEDIPUS

What good will come to them, from having me?

ISMENE

It seems you are a source of strength to them.

OEDIPUS

(Bitterly)

Reduced to nothing, then a source of strength?

ISMENE

The gods who tore you down, will raise you up.

OEDIPUS

A trifle – Tear down youth then raise up age.

ISMENE

Be sure of one thing. Creon will soon be here.

OEDIPUS

Creon? For what purpose?

ISMENE

To fetch you back and hold you in his power –
But not to Thebes itself – to stay nearby.

OEDIPUS

What will they gain by having me near Thebes?

ISMENE

It seems, unless your tomb is properly cared for,
It will bring curses down upon them.

OEDIPUS

It does not take a god to see their purpose.

ISMENE

They want you to be near enough to be
Within their power, but not be your own master.

OEDIPUS

(*Hesitating*)
Do they plan to bury me in Theban soil?

ISMENE

Guilt for the death of Laius would prevent that!

OEDIPUS

No, I'll not let them own this body.

ISMENE

One day those words will cause them grief.

[109]

OEDIPUS

Who told you of these prophecies, my daughter?

ISMENE

Many travellers come from Delphi.

OEDIPUS

(*Softly*)

Has Phoebus Apollo remembered Oedipus?

ISMENE

Those travellers from Delphi say so.

OEDIPUS

Does either of my sons know this?

ISMENE

Father, they both know very well.

OEDIPUS

They fight each other for the crown
Rather than have their father back?

ISMENE

Yes, father, that is so, alas.

OEDIPUS

(*Angry*)

Then may the gods not end their fighting!
Let me foretell the outcome of their war!
Eteocles, who seized the throne, will not retain it!
Nor Polyneices, expelled by him, regain it.
For neither, when I was driven into exile,
Raised a hand to help me.

CHORUS
Oedipus, you yourself sought exile.
Prayed for it to Creon.

OEDIPUS
That is not so. I never asked for exile.
Upon that dreadful day of revelation
That I was the murderer of Laius, I craved
Nothing except to be killed by stoning.
But no one helped me then achieve that end.
The oracle said that I must stay in Thebes.
Then when some time had passed, I felt I had been
Excessive in self-condemnation.
It was then that Creon chose to drive me out.
My sons, who could have kept me in Thebes, did
    nothing.
I wandered through a world that was their lack
Of one kind word, a blind man and a beggar.
It was those girls, my daughters, took care of me.
Their brothers fought between them for my throne.
Neither shall ever have me as an ally
No luck will come to either, crowned or uncrowned.
I know this from the oracles you spoke of
Apollo's blessing promised at my death.
Let them all come, Creon, my sons, all of them,
I shall not favour any. Thebes will fall
And I shall save Colonos from the Thebans.

CHORUS
We begin to feel compassion for you, since
You say that you will save Colonos.
What I shall counsel now is for your good.

OEDIPUS

I'll follow your advice in all you say.

CHORUS

Make atonement to the Eumenides
Into whose sacred ground you trespassed.

OEDIPUS

What rites of penance shall I pay?

(*Soft music during the ensuing passage until exit of* ISMENE.)

CHORUS

First, from a perennial spring
In clean hands to this shrine bring
Water as drink-offering.

OEDIPUS

And when I have obtained that draught?

CHORUS

Take this bowl a master wrought,
Wreathe round its rim new-shorn lamb's wool.

OEDIPUS

And then?

CHORUS

Mix the draught with honey but no wine
Then, with the bowl filled to the brim,
Pour the libation on the soil.

OEDIPUS

And when the earth has drunk it in?

CHORUS

Repeat this prayer to the divine
Goddesses, guardians of the shrine.

OEDIPUS

What prayer? What incantation?

CHORUS

I call upon you spirits, the benign
Guardians of the sacred grove: receive
This contrite suppliant in your healing grace.

OEDIPUS

'This contrite suppliant in your healing grace.'
I am weak and old and blind and cannot go.
Let one of these go. Ismene,
Go for me. The prayers of one,
If they are deeply felt, are prayers of all.

ISMENE

Dear father, I'll go for you. (*To* CHORUS) Show me the
    way,
One of you, guide me there.

(*Exit, with one of* CHORUS. *The stage darkens.* CHORUS *round*
OEDIPUS. *They are suddenly sinister, malign, hissing at him. This
scene is spoken as chanted – a bit surreal.*)

CHORUS

We know that nothing is more dreadful
Than to relive unhappiness
That has been buried under later time.
And yet I long to know.

[113]

OEDIPUS

(*Startled*)
    What?

CHORUS

The story of your crimes and sufferings.

OEDIPUS

Customs of hospitality require
The exile need not tell his shame.

CHORUS

So many different tales are whispered.
I want to hear from you the true one.

OEDIPUS

No!

CHORUS

We gave you sanctuary you sought:
Now grant us what we ask from you.

OEDIPUS

That suffering, that anguish
Was consequent on acts committed by me in utter
    ignorance.
Not one of my own choice.

CHORUS

What acts? What acts? What were they?

OEDIPUS

Thebes bound me by a sinful marriage
To Jocasta, source of all that evil.

CHORUS
Then it is true, as people say,
Your partner in that royal bed
Was your own mother?

OEDIPUS
Your words cast stones at me.
Those children begotten by me on that bed
Are both my sons and my brothers,
Both my daughters and my sisters.

CHORUS
Shameful . . . monstrous . . .

OEDIPUS
Sprung from the same womb
As I myself was born from.

CHORUS
How terrible your sufferings must have been!

OEDIPUS
Unending dark enveloped me.

CHORUS
Sinned too . . . A sinner, aren't you?

OEDIPUS
Never of my own will.

CHORUS
How then? How? How? How?

[115]

OEDIPUS
It was a gift, the crown the Thebans gave me –
I saved them from the Sphinx . . . Would I had never
won it.

CHORUS
(*Closing in on him*)
Then there was blood, wasn't there? Blood?
Blood? Your father's blood?

OEDIPUS
(*Wildly*)
Blood? Blood? Who told you about blood?

CHORUS
Your father's? You shed your own father's blood?

OEDIPUS
Blow upon blow! It is you who murder me!

CHORUS
Murderer. Parricide you are.

OEDIPUS
No! No! No! I have a case to plead.

CHORUS
What case? What case?

OEDIPUS
The man I killed was seeking to kill me.
I did nothing in malice, all in self-defence
A court of law would prove my innocence.

ONE OF CHORUS
Hush. Here comes Theseus, King of Athens.

(*Enter* THESEUS *with guards. He is calm, poised, magnanimous. His words are measured, as though behind them there were the beat of a metronome. He is a bit vain.*)

THESEUS
Oedipus, son of Laius, having heard
From time long past the story of your marriage
And of your cruel loss of sight
And being told that you were here
I have come to see for myself. Seeing
Leaves no doubt that you are who they say –
Those rags, and the gashed eyes, and the scarred face
Declare your name. Looking at you
Compassion precedes every question
Started by curiosity, and asks:
'How can I help you best?', that only.
What do you want of me and Athens
Which brings you here with that girl by your side?
State only your needs. How could I be indifferent to
    them,
I who passed my youth in exile
In scorching deserts and on wild seas – endured
Perils until that time unknown? Never would I
Turn my back on a wanderer like you,
Refusing aid to him.
Hardship has taught me lessons of humanity
And that, despite these trappings of power, I am
Like you, simply a man.
At the end, our two fates are one.

[117]

OEDIPUS
Nobility shines through your words, King Theseus.
You have read my story in my scars.
You leave me here with nothing else to say
But state my needs.

THESEUS
Yes, they are what I want to know.

OEDIPUS
That you accept my body when I die.
Do not reject this hideous gift.
You will benefit with more than beauty from it.

THESEUS
How benefit?

OEDIPUS
Time will make that apparent.

THESEUS
When?

OEDIPUS
After my death, when they have built my tomb.

THESEUS
You jump to that last day. What do you wish
In the time that lies between?

OEDIPUS
Your word that you will build my tomb
Will suffice to span that interval.

THESEUS
It seems very little that you ask.

OEDIPUS
When the time comes, that little may seem much.

THESEUS
You mean, it will bring me trouble with your sons?

OEDIPUS
My sons. They want to take me back to Thebes.

THESEUS
(*Sharply*)
Well, isn't that what you want too?
Home-coming – end to weary exile?

OEDIPUS
When I wished to stay there they refused.

THESEUS
(*A bit impatient*)
Petulance doesn't help you in your case.

OEDIPUS
First let me speak, before rebuking me.

THESEUS
That's reasonable. I am listening.

OEDIPUS
They do not want me in Thebes itself
But near the border, to be in their power.

[119]

THESEUS
Why do they want you there then?

OEDIPUS
The oracle at Delphi prophesied
That if they do not tend my grave
Thebes will be conquered by Athens in war.

THESEUS
Athens and Thebes are at peace now, Oedipus.

OEDIPUS
All between them and you is sunshine now
But time will make it shadow in an instant
And for some trifling cause, unless
What Phoebus prophesies is false.
If the gods do not lie, you would be wise,
King Theseus, to let me stay here.

THESEUS
(*Benevolent*)
You come here as a suppliant to our gods,
And bringing promises to aid us.
Who would reject such friendship? Now I name you
A citizen of Athens, free to live
Here at Colonos. My guard will protect you.
Or live in Athens in my palace.
If you prefer that. Choose.

OEDIPUS
I had forgotten there was magnanimity.
Witnessing gods, love such a man.

THESEUS
Which do you choose?

OEDIPUS
To stay here, at Colonos.

THESEUS
Here? For what reason?

OEDIPUS
To resist my enemies – and yours.

THESEUS
Fear nothing. I shall never fail you.

OEDIPUS
Soon men will come from Thebes to take me.

THESEUS
My guard will protect you, if they come.

OEDIPUS
They'll come as soon as you are gone. I warn you.

THESEUS
Do not instruct me in how to rule.

OEDIPUS
I am afraid.

THESEUS
I, Theseus, know no fear.

OEDIPUS

Because you do not see the danger.

THESEUS

None will take you from here against my will.
Before now, boastful and bragging, enemies
Have threatened me. But where the mind
Is lord of its own inner world, fears vanish.
As for the Thebans, though they swear
They'll seize you as their booty, perhaps the ocean
Will prove too craggy-mountained, and too wide
For them to cross. When I am gone, Oedipus,
My name – Theseus – will suffice to protect you.

(*Exeunt.*)

CHORUS

Stranger, this is shining Colonos,
Famed for horses, loveliest place.
Nightingales pour forth their song
From wine-dark depths of ivy where they dwell
Close to the god's inviolable bowers,
Heavy with fruit and never visited
By scorching sun or rending wind.
Here Dionysus revelling runs
The nymphs that nursed him, his companions.

Each dawn narcissus clusters, washed
In the sky dew, upraise their crowns,
Those worn of old by the great goddesses,
And crocuses like shafts of sunlight show.
Fed by eternal streams, the fountains
Of Cephysus fan through the plains
Bringing their swelling breasts increase,
Nor are the Muses absent from this place.

[122]

And here a miracle, a thing unknown
In Asia, flourishes perpetually –
The self-renewing vast-trunked olive tree,
A bastion for us against enemies
And, for Athenian children, nurturer.
Nor youth nor age can cause it damage
For Zeus smiles on it, and grey-eyed
Athena holds it in her keeping gaze.

But most of all, I have to praise the horse,
Poseidon's gift to this land, glorious,
Running beside white horses of the waves.
And Colonos is where Poseidon taught
Man bit and bridle for the horse the horse
To tame the wild colt and to curb his speed:
And taught him carve the wood for prows and oars
Chasing the Nereids through the waves.

(*Enter* CREON *and* GUARDS.)

CREON

Gentlemen, I see that my appearance here alarms you.
Do not, anyone, be afraid. I come armed, but I have
no intention of using force. I am old, and I respect the
power of Athens.

Old though I am, I have been sent by the citizens
of Thebes (I follow their wishes though I am regent of
Thebes) to plead with that man standing over there to
return to our people, to his family.

The message which I bring from Thebes – one
which I as your brother feel most strongly of all – is
very simple. Just this – 'Come home, Oedipus,
Thebes needs you.' And you – it is evident from just
looking at you – need Thebes. Speaking for myself, it

[123]

breaks my heart to see you standing there, a foreigner
and a vagrant, having to live off the charity of
foreigners, and with only that girl in rags to take care
of you. As for her, I had never dreamt she could sink
so low, doomed always to serve you in your
destitution – a fine wench in the ripeness of her
youth, but not on the marriage market exactly, her
one chance of getting a man being, I should say, some
rough farmhand who, when drunk, might hurl
himself on top of her.

If what I am saying seems blunt – coarse almost –
is not that the result of your situation here? The
spectacle of it is a terrible reproach to you and to her
and to me and to Thebes – the whole lot of us. An
open running sore cannot be concealed. I call upon
you, Oedipus, to co-operate in doing what we can to
draw a veil over scandals by returning to Thebes and
the respectability of your family roof. Take a grateful
farewell of this great prince Theseus for he deserves
the thanks of all of us, then come home with me.
Come back to Thebes, to me, your brother –

OEDIPUS
Liar! Hypocrite! I know your game,
It is to entice me back to Thebes
Which you intend to make my prison:
To end my life in utmost agony.
But you know well that long ago in Thebes
When I had won a little peace of mind
And would have quietly stayed there – then
You drove me into exile – no talk then
Of us two being brothers. Now you see
Me welcome in Colonos, you ask me back
Protesting family affection.

[124]

What once would have been kindness, now
Is cruelty: as though a neighbour
Who never offered help when you most needed it,
When you no longer felt that need, thrust on you
Unnecessary show of help through ill will.
Before all of those here, I say
Creon's intent is not to welcome me
To Thebes, but place me near its borders
And keep me in his power, so Thebes
Escape unharmed in coming war with Athens.
Go back and leave me where I have found sanctuary.

CREON

The years, I see, have failed to teach you wisdom.

OEDIPUS

Nor you that smooth words never wholly can
Disguise your base intentions.

CREON

Some men use many words but miss the mark.

OEDIPUS

As though yours were so true, they hit dead centre.
Go back, go back, where you came from.

CREON

Come of your own free will, or I shall make you.

OEDIPUS

What force is there behind that bragging?

CREON

We already have one of your daughters.
We'll seize the other now. Guards!

OEDIPUS

Ismene? You have taken Ismene?

CREON

Yes. And now we'll take Antigone.

OEDIPUS

Friends, help me. Drive the intruder out.

CHORUS

Out with you! Out!
What you have done and what you purpose doing
Are against the law.

CREON

(*To* GUARDS)

The time has come for you to take that girl by force if
she refuses to go of her own free will.

ANTIGONE

What can I do? Help me!

CHORUS

(*To* CREON)

What are your demands?

CREON

(*Pointing to* OEDIPUS)

Not him. I won't touch him. I ask
Only what is mine already, his daughters
Whom I adopted when he begged me do so.

OEDIPUS

Citizens of Colonos –

CHORUS

(*To* CREON)
Lawless. Violence. Theft.

CREON

Justice is on my side. Those girls are mine, you
entrusted them to me.

OEDIPUS

Oh, Athens! Theseus!

CHORUS

(*As* GUARDS *drag off* ANTIGONE)
What are you doing? Let her go!
Do you want war?

CREON

Do not attempt to stand in my way.

CHORUS

War between Thebes and Athens! Do you want war?

OEDIPUS

What did I prophesy to Theseus?

CHORUS

Men of Colonos come to our support!
Send to Athens for help!
Search out King Theseus and bring him here!

[127]

OEDIPUS
Antigone, Antigone, where are you, my child?

ANTIGONE
They are dragging me away, my father.

CREON
Take her away.

(ANTIGONE *is taken off.*)

(*To* OEDIPUS)
So now you've lost both your crutches. Since you
have wilfully chosen to repudiate your own home and
family I'll leave you to your momentary triumph over
Thebes. Later no doubt you will come to see your
error and realize that now, as so often before, you
harm only yourself by disregarding the advice of your
compatriots, and following your own anger – a sick
counsellor.

(CREON *begins to exit.*)

CHORUS
(*Barring him*)
Stop!

CREON
Take your filthy hands off me!

CHORUS
Not until you release those girls.

CREON

If you don't let me go,
You'll soon have more than them to ask for.
I'll take him too! I'll claim my ugly booty!

CHORUS

Are you threatening us?

CREON

The threat will soon be carried out as deeds.

CHORUS

First you will have to answer to our King.

OEDIPUS

Before he does that, let me speak to him!
I call now on Apollo, who seeing all,
Saw you steal from my dark
Her who is light to me,
To make you at your life's end suffer
Deprivation equalling mine –
Loss of your child and blindness.

CREON

(*To* CHORUS)
See how he foams!
Bear witness all of you.

OEDIPUS

They look at both of us and see
Your threats translated to my agony
My words bite empty air.

[129]

CREON

Well, I'll indulge my temper too,
Old though I am. Guards
Arrest this raging madman!

CHORUS

If you think you can do this in Athens
Creon, you are mistaken.

CREON

I think so. And I can. And I do.

CHORUS

If that were true, there would not be an Athens.

CREON

My cause is just and gives my old age strength.

OEDIPUS

Citizens, did you hear him threaten me?

CHORUS

Threats he will never carry out, the god knows.

CREON

The god may – you don't.

CHORUS

Insolence! Blasphemy!

CREON

How can you insult a man of straw?

CHORUS

Theseus, King of Athens, help!
The enemy stands at the gates,
The Bronze Threshold of Athens.

(*Enter* THESEUS.)

THESEUS

What is this outcry? What reason can be so pressing
As to interrupt me at my sacrifice
To Poseidon, defence of Colonos?

OEDIPUS

Dear friend, I know you by your voice.
Creon has taken away my daughters.

THESEUS

Can this be true?

OEDIPUS

It is as I said.

THESEUS

(*To* ATTENDANTS)

One of you run to the sea-shore and round up those
still making sacrifices.
Collect together cavalry, foot-soldiers, all available
men and despatch them to the frontier to that place
where two roads meet.
Cut the Thebans off there.
Prevent them smuggling the girls into Theban
territory.
I will not be made to appear a fool who lacked
foresight.

[131]

(*Pointing at* CREON)

> And as for him, if I too gave way to ill temper
> I would not let him go from here unharmed.
> But I'll restrain myself to using law
> To hold him who, against the law, holds others.
> You shall not leave the country till these girls
> Are brought before me here and freed.
> Your violent acts disgrace us all.
> You come to Athens where freedom is the law
> And put the law aside and spit on freedom;
> Taking prisoners as your prizes
> As though this land were powerless to resist,
> Its people shadows, I, its King, a nothing.
> Find them and free them. Or we'll take you prisoner.

CHORUS

(*Sneering at* CREON)

> See where your deeds have brought you.
> What will you do now, stranger?

CREON

Great prince, I had no thought of underestimating the
valour of the Athenians when I came here. It is simply
that I could not imagine that they would be so
enamoured of my sister's son who was also her
husband as to give him, a citizen of Thebes, domicile
here, against my will. I felt confident, too, that they
would not wish to entertain a parricide, a man
disgraced by his having carnal intercourse with his
own mother, Jocasta. The laws of Athens do not let go
unhindered parricides and incestuous adulterers.
Even so, I would not have demanded his extradition
had I not heard that this man was abusing his
sanctuary here in order to call down curses on me and

the people of Thebes – his own people. You have just
witnessed an example of his rage.

However, in view of the weakness of my present
position, although I consider that my reasons for
coming here were just, I shall bow to your power. But
old as I am I should give notice that I intend to pursue
the matter after my return to Thebes.

OEDIPUS

Old as you are, you say – whom do you shame
More of us two ancients when you speak of
Parricide, incest, murder?
– Crimes done with no intent on my part,
But visited upon me, who was innocent,
To placate the gods, perhaps, because
From time far back, they were angry with our house.
Apart from them, you can find no sin
In me, alone. How am I guilty
Because an oracle prophesied the doom
That would overtake my father at a son's hand
– I who was then not born, nor even
That father's seed within my mother's womb?
If, being grown to manhood, one day I saw
A stranger at a place where three roads meet
And if that stranger attacked me and I struck
Back at him and killed him, never knowing
He was my father, how am I guilty
Of evil-doing, murder, parricide?

How dare you stand there and name Jocasta,
She who was your own sister. But since you have
   spoken
I'll do so too. Yes, she was my mother
– Which, when we were married, I did not know –

[133]

Nor did she know it – when, to her shame,
She bore children to me – the son she had borne.
We did not will these things. One thing I know,
     though:
That you, of your own free will, with wilful malice,
Will now to calumniate us.
I deny that I was guilty in that marriage
Or guilty of murdering my father,
Those crimes you cruelly accuse me of.
Let me ask you just one thing: supposing
Now, at this instant, a man should walk in here
And try to kill you – you who are so virtuous –
Would you stand stock still and ask: 'Are you my
     father?'
Or would you with one great blow strike him dead?
I think that as you love your life you'd kill him
And not wait on authority to do so.
That was my situation on that morning.
And, were my father alive, he would forgive me.
But you, because you are a politician,
Taunt me with this before all these – your public,
And because you hope to flatter Theseus.
One thing, though, you forget: that this is Athens,
And Athens grants me sanctuary in Colonos.

                    THESEUS
We have promised to protect you, Oedipus, and we
shall keep our promise. Creon, I order you to lead us
to the place where your guards hold his daughters.
We'll take them under our protection. If war is the
consequence we are ready.

                    CREON
Being powerless here, I obey.

THESEUS
The hunter has been hunted, the spoiler despoiled.

(*Exeunt.*)

CHORUS
(*Spoken like members of a crowd watching a sporting event*)
Oh to be out there where the enemy
at bay joins us in battle   oh
to hear the bronze clangour
sword on sword shield on shield sword on shield

would that I were there

But where? Where? Where? Can the fighting be
beside the shore loved by Apollo, or
along those torch-lit beaches where
the terrifying goddesses
perform those terrifying rituals
of which no mortal tells?

Theseus, awake at last to war, will
soon, very soon, greet those two captives,
daughters of Oedipus,
and prove himself the saviour of their lives.

Victory will be ours!
Victory will be ours!
Creon is sure to lose!

Some deep thought in my soul presages
that Creon will receive his wages
for the sin that he has done.

[135]

Oh that I were a dove
able to perch upon a cloud above
the battle and look down
Hate defeated by our victor, Love.

Has the battle yet begun?
Has Creon lost? Has Theseus won?

In my soul I still am certain
the two maidens seized by Creon
Will be back among us soon!

Surely today our god will work some marvellous thing
And that will be the victory of our King

O ruler of heaven, lord of battles, Zeus, and
Pallas Athene and Apollo, grant
that this land's defenders triumph!

Our prayer is granted. Here come
The two girls with their rescuer, Theseus.

(*Enter* ANTIGONE, ISMENE *and* THESEUS.)

ANTIGONE
O father, father, if only you could see
This brave prince, our rescuer.

OEDIPUS
You're back? You're really back? Both of you back?

ANTIGONE
Yes, both. And running to embrace you.

OEDIPUS

If at this moment I should die,
I would die happy.
Tell me, how were you rescued?

ANTIGONE

His was the deed, his be the words.

OEDIPUS

Stretch forth your hand, and touch me, King,
No I had forgotten when I said that,
You should not suffer the polluted thing.

THESEUS

My words found utterance in my deeds.
I kept my promise. Here are your two daughters;
They will have words not mine to tell you later.

OEDIPUS

Prince, in you I find that which I thought
Existed no more in this world.
Fear of heaven, spirit of justice, lips
That do not lie.

THESEUS

I have to tell you what may hurt you.

OEDIPUS

What?

THESEUS

While I was sacrificing to Poseidon,
A man, also a suppliant, entreated me
To let him speak with you.

[137]

OEDIPUS

(*Suspicious*)
What man? Where did he come from?

THESEUS
From Argos. Have you a kinsman there?

OEDIPUS
From Argos? I won't speak with him!

THESEUS
Why? What's the matter?

OEDIPUS
I know that suppliant. Polyneices
My son, leader of brigands.

THESEUS
Piety to the god demands you see him
Since he is a suppliant to Poseidon.

ANTIGONE
Let him come, father.
Hear what he has to say – what harm can that do?
That he has wronged you makes you no less his
    father,
And, as his father, you should not refuse him.
Think of the wrongs done to you by your parents
And of the wrongs that you have done them.
Hear what my brother has to say.

OEDIPUS
Well, I shall see him, though against my will,
To honour Theseus, and for your sake.

[138]

CHORUS

Whoever craves a longer life than his allotted span
That man
I count a fool. For what do more days add
But to his sum of grief, and not of pleasure,
If he endure beyond the appointed measure?

The curtain falls the same, in any case.
When his superfluous days are done,
Youth, wedding, dance, song, death itself
Are one.

Best, never to have been born at all; the next best is
Quick turn back to that nothing whence he came.

For after tasting youth's soon-passed
Feather-head follies, then what troubles
Do not crowd in on him:
Faction, envy, murder, wars, and last
Senility claims its own:
Unsociable,
Infirm, unfriended, shunned by all.

Oedipus is old: a promontory
Exposed on every side to storms
The elemental forces overwhelm,
Every disaster falling on him: come
From sunrise and the sunset, from
The icy north, torrid meridian,
All day – and all night long, the glittering stars.

ANTIGONE

See. Polyneices is coming now.

[139]

(*Enter* POLYNEICES. *While* POLYNEICES *is speaking,* OEDIPUS *seems like a statue, deaf as well as blind to all he has to say.* POLYNEICES *goes round and round this figure trying in vain to evoke some response from him. He gets none until at the end* OEDIPUS *breaks into terrifying speech.*)

POLYNEICES

Which causes me more pain? The wrongs
Done to me by my brother, or this, of seeing
My father stand there, exiled, blind, in rags
So old and scarred they seem his very flesh
And those two girls, my sisters,
His only helpers.
                    Before you all,
Here I confess my crime of callousness
When he was driven from Thebes.
(*To* OEDIPUS)
                              Why don't you say
    anything?
Why do you turn away? Speak! Will you send me
    from here
With nothing but that show of stony scorn
To take with me? Dear sisters,
– Ismene – Antigone – plead with him,
Do not let me go away unanswered,
Dishonoured and disgraced.
(OEDIPUS *is silent.*)
                          Like Theseus, father
I also am a suppliant to Poseidon.

ANTIGONE

Polyneices, go on speaking
Perhaps some word will touch him or at worst
Provoke him to an angry answer.

[140]

POLYNEICES
Father, let me tell you why I have come here.
Like you I am an exile. When you left Thebes,
Being your eldest son, I claimed the throne.

(OEDIPUS *starts forward angrily but does not speak.*)

But then, Eteocles, my brother, drove me out
Having won over the city, not by argument
Nor arms, but in consequence of that curse
Laid on our house by Apollo, I think.
Like you, I was an exile.
Driven out, I went to Argos. There I married
The daughter of Andrastos, and bound to me
By oath the bravest Argive warriors.
I formed, together with them, seven legions.
(Pause.)
Why am I here, you ask? As a petitioner
To you, to help me and my Argive allies,
Seven leaders of seven armies besieging Thebes.
(Pause.)
You'll want to hear their names, surely? First
There's Amphiarus, their swiftest spearsman: then
Tydeus of Aetolia, son of Oneus:
Third, there's Eteoclus, born in Argos: fourth,
Hippomedion whose father Talaos
Sent him, his only son, to join me. Fifth
Capaneus, a man after your heart, father.
He's raring to burn Thebes to the ground.
Sixth, the Arcadian Parthenopaeus.
And last, here am I, your son, their leader.
We all entreat you, father, to deflect
Your wrath from me, your eldest, to its true object
My brother, who drove me, like you, into exile –

[141]

Teiresias prophesies that, with you beside us, we'll
   win.
Like you, I am a beggar and an exile.
Like you, I am dependent on the favour
Of a foreign court, as you are, father, with Theseus.
We've both been driven abroad, far from our home.
While he sits on *our* throne, and sneers at us.
But father, with you as our ally
We'll hurl him from our throne and bring you back
To Thebes, to share the throne, the two of us.
Join us, and what I've said is certain, but
Without you, father, I'll never return alive.

CHORUS

Answer him, Oedipus, not for his sake
But that of Theseus who sent him here as a suppliant.

OEDIPUS

Except for Theseus, I would not say one word.
But now I'll say a few, do him that favour
That will not make him happier in the hearing.
Scoundrel! Traitor! When you wore the crown
Eteocles, your brother, wears today
You drove me, your own father, out of Thebes
To wear these rags you say you weep to see –
Seeing in them yourself as you are now.
It is too late for tears, I will endure
The burden of my remaining as I am
Still, seeing you two brothers as my murderers.
But for my daughters, I would now be dead
Dead of the kindness shown me by these sons.
They are my warriors, my daughters,
My sons are aliens to me, enemies.
My soul has narrowed down to this one thought

[142]

This curse against my sons. You, Polyneices,
Will never overthrow Thebes: nor
Return to Argos. You'll be killed
By your own brother. He'll be killed by you.
Go, tell this to your Argive allies
And let your brother tell his friends in Thebes.
The burning god will carry out the sentence
Oedipus pronounces on his sons.

CHORUS

(*To* POLYNEICES)
Polyneices, we need your company no longer.

POLYNEICES
Alas, for my sad comrades and myself!
This is the end of the long journey
We set forth on, with such high hopes, from Argos.
I cannot tell it to them, nor can I
Turn back to Argos. I must carry on
Silent until the last calamity.
Dear sisters, you who heard my father's prophecies
If they are fulfilled after my death
– As they will be – and you return to Thebes,
Do not dishonour my corpse but give me
Burial with due funeral rites.

ANTIGONE
Polyneices, listen!

POLYNEICES
What is it, Antigone, dear sister?

[143]

ANTIGONE

Go back to Argos with your warriors
Do not destroy yourself and Thebes.

POLYNEICES

How could I ever lead my men again
If they saw me shown to be a coward?

ANTIGONE

Why act in anger? Why sacrifice
Your life? Why destroy Thebes?

POLYNEICES

For shame of being an exile and the object
Of mockery to my brother.

ANTIGONE

Do you not understand? – your actions
Can only make our father's curse come true.

POLYNEICES

I know, but I cannot turn back.

ANTIGONE

Unhappy brother! Who of all your followers
Hearing that prophecy will not forsake you?

POLYNEICES

A good leader does not tell his men bad news.

ANTIGONE

You are set on dying then?

POLYNEICES

Yes, and do not keep me any longer.
It is my fate to travel on that path
Willed for me by my father and the Furies.
But as for you, dear sisters, may the god
Lighten your way if you honour my corpse
With burial rites I asked. Farewell now.
You will never see me again.

(*Exit* POLYNEICES.)

Apotheosis of Oedipus

(*The stage darkens. Thunder and lightning.*)

CHORUS

Once more the voice of doom has spoken
Caused by that blind old vagabond
Unless, indeed, it should betoken
The hour of his approaching end.
For heaven's decrees are never vain.
Time watches today's overthrow
Of fortunes that will rise tomorrow.
Hark, the thunder peals again!

OEDIPUS

Children! Children!
Send quickly now to Theseus.

ANTIGONE

Why, father, do you need him?

OEDIPUS

The thunder is the sign that soon
I must go down among the dead.

CHORUS

Louder and louder, peal on peal!
Always when the heavens break forth
With hail and lightning lashing earth
Some fearful thing is brought to birth.
Some monstrous future time will soon reveal.

OEDIPUS

These portents show my end is near.
No longer can I turn aside from death.

ANTIGONE

What portents, father? How do you know them?

OEDIPUS

I know. I know. Let someone run
Quickly, for Theseus.

CHORUS

The storm roars louder louder all around.
Have pity on us, Zeus. Because
We pitied him on whom you set your curse
Do not deny your mercy to us.
Again. Again. I hear that dreadful sound.

OEDIPUS

Is Theseus near? And when he comes,
Will I be still alive to talk with him?

ANTIGONE
What was your pledge?

OEDIPUS
Recompense for kindnesses he showed me.

CHORUS
Theseus, leave those sacrifices
You make in the glade's deep recesses
To Poseidon, the sea god.
Leave them now, come back to us
For good to recompense the good
That you showed to Oedipus.
Come here quickly, quickly, Theseus.

(*Enter* THESEUS.)

THESEUS
What is the purpose of this summons
Interrupting my sacrifices
Once more, to the sea god – come from
You, my own people, as well as from my guest.
Is it some great disaster the storm caused?
That alone could justify such importunity.

OEDIPUS
It is the god, the god, who summons you.
My life draws to its close. I must requite
Benefits infinite and keep a promise.

THESEUS
What makes you sure this is the end?

[147]

OEDIPUS

The rolling of the thunder and the flashing
Of the reiterated lightning, portents
Of my immitigable death.

THESEUS

You never proved an untrue prophet, friend.
Tell me what you want and I will grant it.

OEDIPUS

To you I will unfold now what will prove
Incorruptible treasure stored for Athens.
Soon without need of any hand to guide me
I'll lead you to the place where I must die.
Never reveal to anyone its secret
Then it will prove a hidden sure defence
Stronger than shields, keener than swords of friends.
Mysteries are here it were profane to name
That you alone will know when you go there.
I cannot speak of them before these people,
Not even these two daughters I so love –
Secrets which you must guard with all your soul
Which, when you die, you'll whisper to your son,
Who, when he dies, will whisper them to his.
Thus you will keep Athens impregnable
From Theban youth sprouting like dragon's teeth.
Let us go now, for the god summons me.
Dear daughters, follow. For mysteriously
I guide you who, before this, were my guides.
Do not touch me. I must go alone
To find that sacred place where I'll be buried.
This way. This way. Now Hermes is my guide
Towards Persephone gathering in the dead.
O light light light! Unseen by me, I feel

[148]

The sun's last warmth a touch upon my hand
While I descend into the shadows.
O Theseus, dearest friend, farewell
Blessed be this country as befits your greatness.

CHORUS

Since I am able to adore
The unseen goddess,
And thee, too, Aidoneus,
Lord of the children of the night,
Hear now my prayer:
That not in pain or with lament
Oedipus may pass the gates
And journey to the fields below,
And enter in the Stygian house.
How many were the causeless sorrows
Came to him in this life, so now
May the god raise him up in death.
And may the Dog, the watcher in the dark,
Leave a clear path for him, the stranger,
Descending to the darkest depths of Hades,
O giver of eternal sleep.

Transfiguration of Oedipus

OEDIPUS

Children, my life ends at the brazen threshold.
I lay down here that burden
Borne by you happily for my sake –
No light one, I well know. And yet one word
Made it seem nothing – love – that which you had
From me unceasingly as from none other –
And will no longer have to light your lives.

[149]

A VOICE

(*From above*)
  Oedipus, Oedipus, why do you delay?

OEDIPUS

(*To* THESEUS)
  Dear friend, now offer your right hand
  To my daughters. Let them take yours.
  Promise to care for them.

THESEUS

  I promise.

OEDIPUS

(*Reaching out towards his daughters*)
  Ismene, Antigone, dear daughters,
  Now summon all your courage,
  Bid me farewell, then go from here alone
  Do not look or listen on your way
  For mysteries unlawful to be known.
  Go. Go. Go. Theseus, you only, stay!
  As is your right, to witness to the end.

(*Exeunt* ISMENE *and* ANTIGONE. *There is a blaze of light, beyond which* OEDIPUS, *transfigured a moment silhouetted against it, becomes invisible.* THESEUS, *with arm raised to shield his eyes from the vision, then turns round.*)

THESEUS

  Light within light, invisible – music
  In music, silence. Calm
  Of utter peace, the god within the storm.
  No violence
  Of thunderbolt, or wave driven inshore,

[150]

Bore him away from us.
It was as if, unseen, a messenger
Come from that other world, without lament
And without pain.
Transformed his death to love, drew him
Out of mortality to the immortal
Life that is only wonder! Oh, my words
Are a child babbling the unspeakable!

(*There is a short blackout. When the light reappears, only the* CHORUS *is on the stage.*)

CHORUS
Where are his daughters? Here they come,
Back to this world of living and lament.

(*Enter* ANTIGONE *and* ISMENE.)

ANTIGONE
Now we are left alone with nothing but
Our father's fate, the doom laid on our house.
For his sake, when he lived, we bore the pain
With no thought but to care for him.
Now all is void, and meaningless.

CHORUS
The blind old wanderer is gone forever.

ANTIGONE
(*Fiercely*)
Yes – as you wished – he is gone. Dead. Dead
Not through accident or war or sickness
But snatched into invisibility
Suddenly by some strange fate.

[151]

How shall we two sisters go on living
Our bitter lives without him
Upon what barren lands or wastes of ocean?

ISMENE

Oh that I could pull death down on me
To join him in the dark where he has gone.
I cannot bear this world of the harsh sun.

CHORUS

Children! Daughters! Best ones! Fate
Must be endured. Do not give way to grief.

ANTIGONE

Past pain now seems lost pleasure. Oh for
That sweetness which seemed such a slight thing then
Of holding him in my embrace. Dear father,
Enclosed forever in eternal dark,
Our love still follows where you are.

CHORUS

He died where he wished – far from Thebes.

ANTIGONE

(*Passionately and wilfully*)
I am seized with such wild longing.

ISMENE

For what, Antigone?

ANTIGONE

To look on the dark house.

ISMENE

What? Where?

ANTIGONE

The dark house of our father.

(ANTIGONE *moves forward.* ISMENE *stops her.*)

ISMENE

That cannot be. That is unlawful.

ANTIGONE

Why do you stand in my way?

ISMENE

He has no tomb. You heard, from what he said.

ANTIGONE

Take me where he is, and let me die there.
From now, death is my home.

ISMENE

Don't go! How could I live without you?

CHORUS

Peace. Peace. Be calm. Here Theseus comes, your
    rescuer.

(*Enter* THESEUS.)

THESEUS

There has been enough of lamentation.
The Eumenides, the dreaded kindly ones,
Guardians of the living and the dead will take offence
If you rebel against their wise decrees.

[153]

ANTIGONE

Theseus, I implore you –

THESEUS

To what purpose?

ANTIGONE

Let me see the place where he is buried.

THESEUS

That would be against his wishes.
He charged me not to tell where he is buried.
He said if I stayed faithful to that pledge
I should possess Athens unconquered.
The god bore witness to my vow of secrecy.

ANTIGONE

Since that is so, I must obey the god.
Send us to Thebes then, so I may prevent
Our brothers murdering each other
According to our father's prophecy.

THESEUS

I shall do that and anything you ask
Which may be pleasing to the dead
And is within the reaches of my power.

ANTIGONE

ANTIGONE

Our wise leader Creon, it seems, has arranged for
one of our brothers – Eteocles – to be buried with
all the funeral rites and ceremony due to the King
of Thebes, to be received with honour by the dead
below. But it is rumoured that he'll forbid anyone
in Thebes to bury, honour or mourn our brother
Polyneices. There will be a proclamation that
Polyneices must be left unburied on the plain
outside Thebes, exposed to the scalding sun all
day, a feast for prairie dogs and desert birds.

Why do you say nothing? Don't you
understand? The edict is meant for us, for you and
me. Creon is coming here to proclaim it and declare
that whoever disobeys will meet death by stoning
in front of all the people.

So there it is. Now we have the chance to show
whether we are of noble blood.

ISMENE

Poor Antigone! If things are as you say, what can
we do?

ANTIGONE

Tell me whether you are willing to help me –

ISMENE

Help you do what?

ANTIGONE
Will you help me lift up the corpse of Polyneices
from the ground, and dig the grave? And then, will
you help me bury our poor brother?

ISMENE
That would be disobeying Creon's edict.

ANTIGONE
Don't you remember what Polyneices said – 'Do
not dishonour my corpse but give me burial with
due funeral rites'?

ISMENE
Creon forbids us to bury him.

ANTIGONE
Creon has no right to keep us from burying our
brother.

ISMENE
Think, Antigone, think. Remember how our father, in
his passion to find out the truth about the death of
Laius, brought ruin upon himself. Remember how he
tore out his eyes. Remember how our mother Jocasta
twisted her dress into a noose and hanged herself.
Think how only yesterday our brothers died, each
butchered in the other's blood. Think – now it's our
turn – ours – unless we stop – stop this machine of
murder. Of course you can defy Creon and carry out
our brother's wishes – and bury him – but don't,
Antigone – stop – if you don't stop, the machine will
go on – and we'll die more miserably than all the rest
– if we defy the edict of Creon. Remember, too, we
are women, used to having all decisions made for us.

Whatever you do – and I pray to the gods of the
underworld to forgive me for doing so – I'm going to
obey Creon's edict. It is stupid to do otherwise.

ANTIGONE

I won't argue. Even if you changed your mind now I
wouldn't want you to go with me. Do as you will. I'm
going to bury Polyneices. I am quite prepared to die as
the result of doing so. I shall sleep beside the brother I
love. In offending against Creon's laws I shall be pure
of any sin against the gods. My duty to the dead is
more lasting than my duty to the living: for I must
dwell with the dead forever. I leave it to you to defy
the laws that are eternal, and obey the laws of the
state, which are ephemeral.

ISMENE

I do not want to defy the laws of god: simply, I am not
strong enough to deny the laws of the state.

ANTIGONE

I shall go now and bury my brother.

ISMENE

Antigone, I'm so frightened for you.

ANTIGONE

Don't worry about me. Take care of yourself. That's
what you're good at.

ISMENE

At least keep what you're going to do a secret. And so
will I.

ANTIGONE

Don't. Shout it from the rooftops. If you keep silent,
Creon will accuse you of collusion with me.

ISMENE

You have a heart of fire for deeds of ice.

ANTIGONE

I try to please whom god bids me please – the dead.

ISMENE

You please no one by attempting the impossible.

ANTIGONE

Well, when my strength gives out I'll fall.

ISMENE

A hopeless task should not be undertaken.

ANTIGONE

If you go on talking like that I'll start hating you. And
the dead will hate you too – for eternity. Now leave
me alone in my folly to do my mad act. Nothing is so
shameful as a coward's death.

ISMENE

Go then, if you must. But remember, Antigone,
wherever you go the love of those who love you goes too.

(*Enter* CHORUS.)

CHORUS

SUN!   Brightest ray that ever shone on Thebes
        risen above her glittering streams
        golden eye of dawn beholding

in headlong flight the knight of the white shield –
power-drunk Polyneices come from Argos
    proud in his brilliant panoply!

He like a screaming vast white eagle flew
    against our land
the pinions of his wings   his warriors' shields
his crest   their helmets' plumes
    hovered above our homes
circled around our Seven Gates
      spears thirsting for our blood –

    was driven back before
his foam-flecked beak could nestle in our flesh
his talons fasten on our battlements
So loud our clash of armour at his back
our seething thousand-headed dragon horde!
    Zeus, who utterly abhors
      the prating proud with braggart tongues
      when he perceived that clashing torrent
      onrushing pride of clanging gold,
         struck down with a thunderbolt
         their foremost warrior headlong from
         the topmost rung, his ladder
         pressed against our parapet.

      He crashed to earth torch still ablaze
      his mouth wide open in mid-shout
      his boast of VICTORY cut off
      put paid to all his hopes of conquest.

    Thus Seven Captains at our Seven Gates
    yielded to Zeus their shattered trophies
All but that brother and that brother

[161]

Eteocles and Polyneices
who set their spears against each other
and shared one death willed by their father.

So let us all join hands rejoicing
forget the wars
ignore our scars
visit the temples of the gods   bringing
our thanks to them dancing and singing
ecstatic led by Bacchus in our revelling.

(*Enter* CREON, *attired in gold.*)

CREON
(*Pompous, statesmanlike, buoyant*)
Gentlemen, the ship of state, buffeted
For many years by stormy seas,
Has now once more been steadied by the gods
And brought to harbour on an even keel.
Out of all the citizens of Thebes,
I have summoned you who are here, because
You were loyal to Laius, when he ruled,
And, during his short reign, to Oedipus,
Then, after him, to both his sons,
And, when Polyneices rebelled
And fled to Argos, to King Eteocles.
Since those two brothers now have died together
In tragic circumstances, mutual murderers,
I, as eldest of the house of Labdacus,
Brother of Queen Jocasta, am your King,
Sole heir to the throne, in sole power – at last.
No man, I think, can fully realize
All his potentialities of mind and body
Unless he holds supreme office

[162]

As ruler and lawgiver. For if then
He does not dare put in effect
His declared principles, but remains silent
Through fear, he is seen to be unworthy.
And if he is more loyal to his friends
Than to his country, seen to be corrupt.
I swear to Zeus before you all – I'll not be silent
If I see ruin coming to my country.
And if I have to choose between my country
And my friend, I'll always choose my country.
Our country is the vessel that bears us all,
And only if it is sound can we have friends.
These then are my principles. It is in
Accordance with them now, that I pronounce
This edict concerning the disposition
Of the remains of the sons of Oedipus.

First – for Eteocles who died gloriously
Defending Thebes – every ritual
Befitting to his rank and heroism.
Second – for his brother Polyneices
Who, bringing back with him from exile,
His Argive band of brigands, sought
To destroy Thebes, his native city, his home,
Putting to sword and fire the altars
Of his father's gods; slaughtering his own flesh and
    blood
And making slaves of those he did not slaughter,
This is my edict: Polyneices will receive
No burial, no mourning and no tomb –
But be put out to lie unburied,
Cadaver birds and dogs devour,
Spectacle of disgrace before the sun god.
In this I put my principles in practice

ANTIGONE

Let no one suppose word or act of mine
Will judge the wicked equal with the good.
But he who wills the good of Thebes
I'll honour in his life and after death.

CHORUS

Such is your decision, Creon –
To honour friends and to dishonour foes
Whether among the living or the dead.
And you have the power to carry out your edict.

CREON

Then see to it that you obey my orders.

CHORUS

To carry them out is work for younger hands than
ours.

CREON

Soldiers have been sent to guard the corpse.

CHORUS

What more do you require of us?

CREON

Let no one oppose my edict which is law.

CHORUS

O King, we are not in love with death.

(*Enter* GUARD.)

CREON

Who is this interloper?

[164]

CHORUS

One of the guards of Polyneices' corpse,
Choking with news that he's too scared to utter.

GUARD

I'm not saying I got here as quickly as I might have
done, sir. For all the time while I was coming I was
thinking to myself, 'You fool, you're running to your
certain death when King Creon hears the news you
have to tell him.' Thinking that made me turn around
and start running back but no sooner had I done that
than I started thinking: 'If King Creon was to know
that you was loitering then you'd be for it.' And then I
started running forward again but soon I was having
that first thought again and started running back. So
there I was, running round in circles. And I only got
here because at the end I started saying to myself:
'What happens happens. It's all fate, soldier, fate.'

CREON

(*Sneering*)

What causes all this mental perturbation?

GUARD

I didn't do it, sir, I didn't do it. That's the first thing I
have to say. I didn't see who did do it either. Not one
glimpse. It wouldn't be fair if I was punished.

CREON

Well, you seem to have anticipated every possibility of
your being incriminated.

(*Shouting*)

Now – out with it! – what have you been up to my
man? Evidently you have got some tale that you've
concocted to tell us.

[165]

GUARD

(*Starting to leave*)
I can't say . . . the words choke me. I'm going . . .

CREON

Stop him! Out with it, man, and then get out!

GUARD

It's that corpse, sir. Someone's buried it. Well, not
exactly buried. More like sprinkled a little dust over.

CREON

WHAT! BURIED POLYNEICES! Who would dare do such
a thing?

GUARD

That's just what we were asking. We didn't hear no
tic-tac of an axe, no scratch-scratch nor thump-thump
of a pick or a spade. Not a sound. We didn't see
nothing neither. There weren't no tracks in the dust
like of a wheelbarrow nor a footmark. When the first
watch went out at dawn and came back and told us
about it, we couldn't believe our eyes. Just a light
sprinkling, like I said, of dust over the body covering it
with a veil which seemed to protect it, like magic. No
dog, no bird, had so much as taken a peck at him.

Then we all started quarrelling, cursing and
accusing each other. There wasn't a man of us but
swore he hadn't done it.

Then the soldier who'd first seen the body told us
we had to report the matter to you. That terrified us
most of all and we started quarrelling among ourselves
worse than ever about who should go. Finally, we
drew lots. I was the unlucky one. That's why I'm here.

[166]

CHORUS
There must have been a spell cast by a god.

CREON
(*Enraged*)
Hold your tongue, or you will drive me mad
With rage at your senile imbecility.
It is intolerable to suggest
The gods would wish that we should honour
A traitor come to burn
Their temples, sack this city,
Overthrow their own laws, their creed.
Do you suppose the gods support the wicked?
No, from the first of my rule there have been malcontents
Who muttered at my edicts, wagged their heads
And would not meekly bend their necks under
The yoke of wise authoritative government.
It's they who must have bribed the guards.
For bribed they were I'm certain – no doubt of it.
Money's the greatest evil known to men.
It lays low cities, drives men from their homes,
Corrupts the innocent to crooked ways
Opening young futures on to godlessness.
(*To* GUARD)
If you don't find the culprit now – at once! –
And bring him here before me, death
Will seem a treat to you.
I'll have you made to talk then hang you up
On hooks to teach you what reward
You get from me for taking bribes.

GUARD
Am I allowed to put a word in here
Or should I make myself scarce now?

[167]

CREON

Can't you see your presence maddens me?
You're a born babbler, that's quite clear.

GUARD

Could be whatever you say, but one thing's sure
I never took a bribe from anyone.

CREON

I say you took bribes and you'll pay for it.

GUARD

A pity our chief judge misjudges so.

CREON

Think what you like about my powers of judgement
But you'll have your last judgement coming to you
Unless you find who buried Polyneices.

(*Exit* CREON.)

GUARD

You'll never see me come back, alive or dead.

(*Exit* GUARD, *running*.)

CHORUS

Many are wonders and none more wondrous
Than man with skill to cross the ocean,
Harnessing the gales and driving
A path through storm-grey seas that threaten
From all sides to engulf him. Earth,
The mother of the gods, and inexhaustible,
He furrows with his ploughs drawn by young colts
To and fro, year on year, engraved with lines.

The whistling race of birds, and tribes
Of wild life, and fish harvested,
He snares in nets he wove, so cunning is he.
And through his craft he masters that fierce beast
The lion roaming in the hills and forests.
He puts the halter round the horse's neck
And rings the nostrils of the angry bull.

Words and quick thought and how to rule the city
He's taught himself: and to take refuge from
The icy arrows of the rain and hail.
He has devices to meet all occasions.
With many ruses that can trick diseases,
Only against death he fights in vain.

Ingenious beyond dreams, his diverse skills
Lead sometimes towards good, sometimes bad, ends.
When he obeys the law and honours justice,
His obligation to the gods, the city
Can lift its head in pride: but he who sins
Makes himself of no city citizen
Nor shall he share my home nor share my thought.

(*Re-enter* GUARD *running, dragging* ANTIGONE *after him.*)

GUARD

Here she is, the one what did it. Caught her in the act
of burying him. Where's that King? I want my reward.

(*Enter* CREON.)

CREON

What is the cause of all this uproar?

[169]

GUARD

Well, well, King Creon, here I am again – I who said
I'd never come back, dead or alive. Shows you,
doesn't it, I eat my words. Well, this time we didn't
have to cast no lots, she was my booty, and I claimed
my right to bring her to you, though it did mean
breaking my word. There she was, decorating the
corpse – caught red-handed. Question her,
cross-examine her – she's yours. Treat her gently
though, poor waif.

CREON

How and where did you capture the prisoner?

GUARD

She was burying the corpse. That's what I said, didn't
I?

CREON

You must state the exact circumstances and all the
details.

GUARD

When we got there – with all those ugly threats from
you still ringing in my ears – we swept the corpse all
nice and tidy and cleared all the dust from the skin.
Then we spread ourselves out on a nearby hillock, to
the windward, to avoid the stench. Everyone of us
was wide awake, what with cursing at each other.

Well we went on sitting there, getting hotter and
hotter as the sun rose higher and higher. Then, about
midday, a whirlwind lifted a great cloud of dust from
the plain, covering every leaf of grass, and choking
us.

When, after a long time, the storm had passed,
we opened our eyes and who should we see but this
girl running round and wailing like some bird which
has lost its nestlings. So she, when she saw her
brother's corpse exposed naked out there shrieked
and cried and called down curses on Creon. Then she
poured water from a pitcher she was carrying on to
the head of her brother as a libation.
    Well, we rushed forward and took her prisoner.
She didn't seem at all surprised to see us or try to run
away. We charged her with her crime and she didn't
deny one thing. This made me a bit unhappy because
I couldn't help liking the girl: but not so unhappy for
her as I felt happy on my own account for having
captured my booty – I get a reward don't I?

CREON

Well, you'll get your reward. And now – get out.

(*Exit* GUARD.)

(*To* ANTIGONE)

You, you with your eyes fixed on the ground, look me
in the face and answer. Do you agree with this man's
story or do you deny it?

ANTIGONE

I don't deny one word of it.

CREON

Were you aware that an edict had been pronounced
forbidding anyone to bury Polyneices?

ANTIGONE

How could I not be? It was shouted from the rooftops.

CREON

So you acted in full knowledge that you were breaking
my law?

ANTIGONE

Yes, because I do not consider that your law overrules
the laws of the gods. Even if I were afraid of the
consequences of breaking your law, I'd be even more
terrified of breaking theirs.

I know how to die, with or without your edicts.
And I count it a blessing to die sooner rather than
later. How could a daughter of Oedipus think
otherwise?

What you do now to make me suffer does not
matter. But if I allowed my brother's corpse to lie out
there unburied, that would matter. Perhaps you may
think my actions foolish, but perhaps it is a fool who
judges them.

CREON

(To CHORUS)

Over-stubborn spirits are easiest to tame.
Brittle iron tempered in the hottest fire
Snaps or cracks sooner than the malleable.
The will of wild mares breaks under the curb.
This filly was already insolent
When she broke my law; having done which
She adds worse insult to exalt her deed.
Were she to succeed in this and triumph
Without being punished, I would not be a man.
Although she is my sister's child,

Nearest of my relatives still living
I will not spare her, nor her sister
Who doubtless was a sharer in the plot.
Send for Ismene.

ANTIGONE

Do you plan anything for me worse than death?

CREON

Death will suffice. That's all that I require.

ANTIGONE

Why delay then? I find in your words
Nothing that pleases me, and I hope you find
Nothing that pleases you in mine.
Oh, but for glory! How could I find
A nobler death than this, for burying
My brother? All of you here, if you dared say so,
Approve my deed, but your lips are sealed.
A king has power to make his court a prison.

CREON

(*Ironically*)
I doubt if all here would agree. Did not Polyneices
Wish to put this city to the sword?

ANTIGONE

That did not mean he stopped being my brother.

CREON

Your father said Polyneices was his murderer.

ANTIGONE

My father, where he is now, would not say that.

[173]

CREON

In the world below, do you think Eteocles
And Polyneices held in equal honour?

ANTIGONE

The gods ask the same funeral rites for both.

CREON

One was a patriot, the other was a traitor.

ANTIGONE

Who knows but both seem equal there below?

CREON

My enemy does not become my friend
By virtue of being a ghost.

ANTIGONE

It is my nature to love not hate.

CREON

Get gone then to the world of ghosts
And if you needs must love, love them.
But while I'm in the world above
I will not be ruled by a woman.

(ISMENE *is led in. She is weeping.*)

You – you – who like a viper
Lurked in my house, draining my life-blood
While I was harbouring two pests, unknowing
They would rebel against me – look straight at me –
Do you deny your part in this
Plot for burying Polyneices?

[174]

ISMENE
If Antigone will let me, I confess
My guilt, and hope to share her punishment.

ANTIGONE
To punish you would be unjust. I did it.

ISMENE
If you suffer I want to share your suffering.

ANTIGONE
The dead bear witness I did it alone.
I do not love a partner in words, not deeds.

ISMENE
Do not reject me, Antigone. Let me die.
I also honoured our dead brother.

ANTIGONE
You cannot share my death and should not claim
Credit for acts you never did.

ISMENE
What could life be for me without you?

ANTIGONE
Ask Creon. His laws provide your circumstances.

ISMENE
Why do you mock me? Does it help you?

ANTIGONE
No, it hurts me too.

ISMENE

How can I help you? Even now?

ANTIGONE

Save yourself. Go out of here and live.

ISMENE

Cannot I stay and share your fate?

ANTIGONE

You choose to live. I choose to die.

ISMENE

At least you did not choose with my approval.

ANTIGONE

One world approves your choice, another mine.

ISMENE

I am guilty too. I loved my brother.

CREON

One of these girls was always a rash fool.
Now the other one wants to be one too.

ISMENE

How can I live if she's no longer present?

CREON

Don't speak of the present. She belongs to the past.

ISMENE

(*To* CREON, *bitterly*)
Will you kill the bride of Haemon, your own son?

Entre

CREON
There is other flesh for him to plough.

ISMENE
He'll never find a love like hers.

CREON
He must not marry an evil woman.

ANTIGONE
Haemon, hear how your own father speaks of you.

CHORUS
(*To* CREON)
Will you deny your son the bride he loves?

CREON
Not I, but death will stop their marriage.

CHORUS
You are determined on her death then?

CREON
Determined, yes. Be very sure of that.
Guards, take them to prison.
Treat them as women, though they argue like men.

CHORUS
Happy are those who never tasted evil.
For once a house incurs the rage of heaven
The indignant curse fallen on it never ceases
But remains always, and for ever passes
From life to life through all its generations.

[177]

So from the earliest times the sorrows
Of children of the house of Labdacus
Heap on their dead new sorrows always
Never set free by later generations,
And if a son arise to free that house
A god arises soon to cast him down.

Just as when howling gales from off-shore
Pile up in mountainous waves the Thracian seas
Fathoms above the shadowy sea floor,
These suck up from the depths black sands
Which, risen, spread over all the surface,
While the storm roars against the headlands.

Now of the house of Oedipus, that hope
Which was the last extension of the root,
That light which promised so much is put out
By bloodstained dust that was a debt
Unpaid to the infernal gods,
And by a young girl's frenzied heart.

(*Enter* HAEMON.)

CREON

Well, Haemon, my boy, have you come to upbraid
your old father now that you've heard of the death
sentence being passed on your bride? Or to assure me
that in all circumstances, whatever I do, I shall always
meet with your approval?

HAEMON

Father, I am your son, and whatsoever rules you lay
down for me I'll always follow them. No marriage
could matter more to me than your approval.

[178]

CREON

Yes. That should be your rule in life – obey your father.
There's no more dreadful affliction for a parent than
having disobedient children. They bring trouble to him
and pleasure to his enemies. And don't, for the sake of
sensual pleasure, put aside good judgement on account
of a woman. That's a passion that soon turns cold in the
arms of one who's a bad lot. If you take my advice, you'll
look on this woman as your worst enemy. Let her go and
find a husband down there among the shadows. In the
whole of Thebes she's the only person who's been
caught flagrantly disobeying my edict about the burial of
her brother. I've publicly announced that the
punishment for this is death and I'm not going to go
back on my word before the whole city.

And even should she appeal to me on the grounds
that she is of the same royal blood as I myself – I shall
answer that if I tolerate evil when it is done by my blood
relations then I would also be bound to tolerate it when
done by those not my relations.

In the state, as in the family circle, disobedience is
the worst of evils. Disobedience ruins cities, makes
home a desolation, dissolves ties of loyalty. Take any
citizen who has a satisfactory life and I'll warrant you
that the greater part of his happiness derives from his
obeying the law. We have to support law and order, my
boy; and that means above all on no account letting us
men be guided by women.

CHORUS

Unless senility has robbed us of our wits
What you say makes good sense to us.

HAEMON

Father, the gods have given every human being some
minute portion of reason – the highest thing we can
call our very own. I'm not clever enough, nor do I
wish, to point out anything irrational in what you say.
And yet someone cleverer than I might find
something to criticize in it. I know this because,
purely on your behalf, I keep my ears open to what
people are saying – things no one would dare say to
you. Sometimes I hear people murmuring in the dark
when I walk through the streets of Thebes. And what
they're saying, father, is this: that no woman was ever
condemned more unjustly, more shamefully, for acts
that cover her in glory. When her brother had fallen in
a family quarrel – they say – she wouldn't leave him
unburied, to be torn to pieces by dogs and birds of
prey. Does not she then deserve to be honoured?

For me, father, nothing matters so much as my
father's good name. I beg you then, father: don't
follow the dictates of your anger; don't be certain that
in every instance your word and yours only must be
right. Listen, father: whenever someone thinks that he
alone is wise and that no one else can ever be in a
position to criticize him, that person only shows that
he has a soul which, when put to the test, is found to
be empty.

However wise a man may be it is no disgrace for
him to learn from, and sometimes even to yield to,
argument.

CHORUS

Creon, you may benefit by paying heed to him.
Haemon, you may learn too, from your father.

CREON

Is a man of my age to take lessons from a boy?

HAEMON

Yes, if that boy should happen to talk sense.

CREON

Is it good sense to take sides with a law-breaker?

HAEMON

I do not side with someone who does evil.

CREON

Is not that girl's treachery evil?

HAEMON

No one in Thebes would take that view.

CREON

Is Thebes to tell me how to rule?

HAEMON

Who is it now who's talking like a boy?

CREON

Am not I, as the ruler, the sole judge
Of measures I must take to rule the city?

HAEMON

You would be, if you were its sole inhabitant.

CREON

Is not the city the ruler's property?

[181]

HAEMON
Yes, if he is the ruler of a desert.

CREON
(*To* CHORUS)
This boy, it seems, is champion of a girl.

HAEMON
Yes, if you are a girl – I champion you.

CREON
You openly oppose your father then?

HAEMON
Only when he opposes justice.

CREON
Am I wrong to guard my power jealously?

HAEMON
Yes, if you overrule that of the gods.

CREON
All this adds up to is your plea for that girl.

HAEMON
Plus you plus me plus Thebes.

CREON
You'll never marry her this side of the grave.

HAEMON
If she dies, there'll be two of us the other side.

CREON
You dare to threaten me with death?

HAEMON
Is it a threat to say I'll die if she dies?

CREON
You'll still live to regret this youthful madness.

HAEMON
If you were not my father, I'd say it is you who were
   mad.

CREON
You'll pay for saying that at once.
Bring that detested whore here. Let him see
Her die before his eyes, beside her bridegroom.

HAEMON
I'll never see her die before my eyes
And you, with your eyes, will never see me again.

(HAEMON *rushes out.*)

CHORUS
Creon, your son has rushed out in rage.
The young, stung by harsh words, can do rash deeds.

CREON
Let him be stung to do or dream
Whatever he likes – good luck go with him.
But I'll not spare those girls!

CHORUS

Are you determined then they both must die?

CREON

No, not the other one, Ismene, who's innocent.
You are right to bring that to my mind.

CHORUS

What fate do you plan for Antigone?

CREON

My guards will take her up a lonely path
And shut her in a cave hewn in the rock
With food and drink equal to that religion
Prescribes as bare necessity, so as not to bring
Disgrace on Thebes. She can spend her days in prayer
There, to the gods of the underworld who are
The only ones she worships. In due course
She may be pardoned by me, when she has learned
That emptying libations on the corpses
Of traitors to their country is wasted effort.

(*Exit* CREON).

CHORUS

Love! all-conquering love,
Wrecker of great fortunes, keeper
Of watch all night upon a girl's soft cheek –
Voyager to wild shores, pitching his tent
There, among the uncouth inhabitants:
No god, no man, escapes you, and there is
For him that you enslave, sheer madness.
Through love, the justest and the wisest even
Are corrupted and brought down to ruin.

[184]

Look! In this fight between father and son, victory lies
In the light which love lit in a young girl's eyes –
A fire as fierce as heaven's eternal laws,
Venus unassuageable her force.

(ANTIGONE *being led to her death. In the first part of this scene,*
ANTIGONE *is transfigured, almost chanting her lines.*)

ANTIGONE

Behold me, fellow citizens of Thebes,
Looking on the sun for the last time.
Death, that brings to all eternal sleep,
Brings me who am still living, to its shore.
I shall not be a partner in that dance
Bringing the bridegroom to the bride.
My bridegroom is the lord of the dark lake.

CHORUS

(*Ironic*)

Glorious in your sacrifice, much praised,
You go down to the chasm of the dead.
No wasting illness nor sharp-piercing sword
Has killed you. Mistress of your own fate,
While still alive, you meet the death you chose.

ANTIGONE

I have heard tell of Niobe, that goddess
Chained on the mountain peaks. Like ivy
Rocks, up-twining, covered and enclosed her.
And the rains did not fail nor did the snow
To fall upon her stony tomb
Within which her own tears bedewed her.
My fate appears to me like Niobe's.

ANTIGONE

(*Mocking openly now*)
> She was a goddess, as we know, immortal,
> Born of the gods. We, though, are merely mortal,
> And born of men. It must be comforting
> Though, for a mortal, doomed to mortal death,
> To see her fate in an immortal goddess.

ANTIGONE

> You mock me, mock me. Can you not,
> Respected, virtuous, pious fellow Thebans
> Restrain your sneering till I'm gone?
> Must you laugh at me to my face?
> O sacred stones of Thebes, with chariots
> Crowding your streets, may you, at least,
> Witness my passing hence unwept of friends,
> I without home among the dead or living,
> Condemned by Creon's law, and entering
> This rock-hewn vault, my prison and my tomb.

CHORUS

> Of your own will, you hurled yourself against
> Immutable justice, and you fell: perhaps
> In retribution for your father's crimes.

ANTIGONE

> Your words reach to my bitterest thought, arousing
> Ever-renewed tears for my father
> And all that doom, the house of Labdacus.
> Tears for the horror of the wedding bed
> In which the mother slept beside the son,
> Her husband – marriage out of which I sprung –
> My family to which I now return –
> Accursed – unwed – to them among the shadows.

[186]

He whom I sought to honour in his death,
My brother Polyneices, is my murderer.

CHORUS

Your godliness deserves our praise: and yet
Rebellion against power cannot be tolerated
By him who rules as king: nor is the anger
Inherited by you from your father.

ANTIGONE

Unwept and unbefriended, I am led
Weeping on this journey that no more
Can be delayed. No longer shall I see
The morning star awake the dawn's first light.

(*Enter* CREON. *With his entry the dialogue ceases to be hallucinatory, dream-like.*)

CREON

Do you not understand – self-pitying dirges
Sung by her doomed to die, will never cease
So long as they postpone the end?
Take her away, and having shut her in
Her stony tomb, let her herself decide
Whether she wants to die, or else to live
Forever there. My hands are clean of this.
One thing is certain though: that if she chooses
Life, she'll live enclosed in endless night.
Imprisoned in blindness that was her father's.

ANTIGONE

Tomb, rocky chamber, bridal vault,
This stony path I follow to my own
My family, Persephone already

[187]

Has gathered to the dead: of which I am
The last and the unluckiest, going before
My life achieved its flowering. I pray
My homecoming prove pleasing to my parents
And Polyneices, whose grey corpse
I washed, and poured libations over.
In honouring him, I honoured heaven's laws
For doing which, I now have my reward.
You who are wise will judge I acted rightly . . .
And yet . . . had I been married, with a husband,
And were the mother of his children,
And if that husband, Haemon, lay unburied
Out on the plain, exposed to the raw sky,
I never would have broken Creon's edict.
In that case, though what law would I have followed?
Nature's munificence my law!
My husband dead, I would have found another,
My children dead, I would have had more children.
But with both parents dead, and Polyneices
Dead – all our house dead – honouring him
Became the law and centre of my life.
For obeying which, Creon now condemns me
To follow where there'll be no marriage feast,
No bridegroom, children, bringing laughter.
Yet how have I offended against heaven?
What god can I now turn to, I, – men call
Wicked for being virtuous? Perhaps
When I am dead, some god will tell me
What crime I did for which I pay so dearly.
But if the wickedness was Creon's
I could not wish him heavier punishment
Than this he gives me for obeying heaven.

CHORUS

Still the same fury raging through her veins
As once raged through her father's.

CREON

All the more reason that the guards should hurry.

ANTIGONE

Yes, hurry, hurry! Creon commands
That you should hurry! Oh my fellow Thebans
Look the last time upon your last princess
Last of the house of Labdacus
Led to her death because she feared
Heaven's laws more than those of men.

(*She is led away.*)

(*Enter* TEIRESIAS *and* BOY.)

TEIRESIAS

King of Thebes, this boy and I come linked together
Like an infant on all fours – four-legged man –
So the blind walk with one the eyes for two.

CREON

Ancient Teiresias, what brings you here?

TEIRESIAS

To give you the advice you stand in need of.

CREON

When did I ever not heed your advice?

ANTIGONE

TEIRESIAS

When you did so you have ruled wisely.

CREON

(*Ironically*)
My deeds bore witness to your wisdom.

TEIRESIAS

(*Prophetic warning*)
Thebes stands again at the edge of the abyss.

CREON

What do you mean? I tremble at your words.

TEIRESIAS

Learn from signs I interpret by my art.
Today when I was at the altar stone
To which birds fly down at my bidding
I heard their choiring change to clangour
A squalling making chaos out of sense
In its cacophony. With spurred talons
And whirring wings they flew to kill each other.
Fearful, I tried to make the sacrifice
Kindling twigs on the altar, but the god
Of fire refused to set the wood alight.
Gouts of water, spurting steam, gushed from
The flesh on thigh bones, oozing forth
And spluttering on the sodden embers.
The sacrifice had failed to yield a sign;
As this boy – seeing for me as I for others – told me.
You, Creon, have brought back the plague to Thebes!
The hearths and altars of the city
Are tainted by the gobbets of the corpse
Of Polyneices, son of Oedipus,

[190]

Dropped there by dogs and ravens. The gods
Reject our prayers and sacrifices,
Our offerings of polluted flesh.
The whistling of birds is raucous with
The clots of murdered human blood.
Stop, my son, stop. Think. Do not go on.
All men are prone to error, but the man
Who having erred, corrects the evil done
Bettering his course, is wise.
Curb your self will, do not murder
Polyneices in the world below.
My warning still can save you if you heed it.

CREON

(*Deliberately blasphemous and obscene*)
Still trying out on me your ancient trade
Of prophecy, that stinking fish.
Go, trade such trash in India for nuggets
Of filigree in Sardis, but you'll not
Browbeat me into burying Polyneices:
No, not though Zeus's eagles should fly up
Shitting their master's throne and bearing
Tidbits of Polyneices in their beaks.
Not even for fear of such defilement
Of Zeus (whom no man can defile)
Would I grant that traitor burial rites. Beware
You venerable old fraud – if the sage sells his wisdom
For pelf, he'll find he's ridden to a fall.

TEIRESIAS
Alas, who ever knows, who ever thinks . . .

[191]

CREON

(*Mocking*)
Now what wise saw will fly out of that mouth?

TEIRESIAS

How precious, more than gold, are words when wise.

CREON

(*Mimicking him*)
How fatal more than death is arrogance.

TEIRESIAS

Yes, that is what men will soon be saying of you.

CREON

You dreamers always dream too much of money.

TEIRESIAS

You'll taunt me into telling you the truth.

CREON

Tell it then, but please don't ask a fee.

TEIRESIAS

I'll tell you the worst, then, and that scot free.

CREON

Whatever it is, it will not change my mind.

TEIRESIAS

Phaeton's chariot will not have run
Three times around the heavens before
The son sprung from your loins will be
A corpse changed for two bodies – that of her,

Antigone, you thrust into the night,
A living soul entombed in a rock cave,
And that of Polyneices, left unburied
Out on the scorching plain, withheld from those
To whom his soul is due, the infernal gods.
For this, the Eumenides, the avenging Furies,
Lie in wait to tear you into pieces.
Since you have mocked me, hear these words as
    arrows
Aimed at you, my target, from my heart.
Boy, take me away, let us leave him
To hurl obscenities at younger men
Than I, until, at last, he learns perhaps
To be more temperate in speech and have
Greater humility than he shows now.

(*Exeunt* TEIRESIAS *and* BOY.)

CHORUS
Creon, Teiresias has departed
Making dire prophecies,
Coming from him who never has proved wrong.

CREON
I know it well, and am much troubled.
How dreadful to admit that I was wrong,
Yet still more dreadful if his words prove true.

CHORUS
Creon, wait. Listen. Stop. Take advice.

CREON
What shall I do? I'm trembling. Tell me, and I'll do it.

[193]

ANTIGONE

Go! Free Antigone! Creon!
Creon, build a tomb for Polyneices!

CREON
How hard to quell my pride, my stubborn heart.
But I'll obey.
It's unwise to defy god's prophet.

CHORUS
Go, do these things yourself, don't wait on others.

CREON
I'll go immediately, just as I am.
Come with me, guards, fetch spades and pick-axes.
We'll break through walls of rocks to free her.
I myself, King Creon, will do it with my bare hands.
I repent of what I have done. I'll change my life.

(*Exit* CREON.)

CHORUS
O many-named, child of Zeus, Bacchus,
Dweller in Thebes, city of the Bacchantae,
Beside the smoothly flowing river Ismenus,
Near where the dragon's teeth were sown,
Above the crested twin peaks you have seen
The nymphs your worshippers move in procession
With flames of torches glowing through their smoke.

O come from hills of Nysa, ivy-covered,
And from the slopes green with your vines
Here where you're sung with voices more than mortal

You who above all cities honour Thebes,
Now we are once more stricken with the plague,
Return again and save us Bacchus
For whom the stars move and their breath is fire.

(*Enter* MESSENGER.)

MESSENGER
Citizens of Thebes, descendants of Cadmus!
In human affairs, there is no certainty.
Fortune lifts men high then casts them down.
Consider Creon: he was fortunate
In all whereby I judge men to be so.
He saved Thebes from the Argive enemy.
He was the unchallenged ruler of this land.
He reigned in great magnificence and had
Haemon, his heir, a gentle loving prince.
Now all is lost. For when a man's deprived
Of all that brought to him spontaneous joy,
I count him nothing but a breathing corpse.
Palace and storehouses may bulge with treasure
And he be dressed from head to foot in gold,
And yet I would not wish to be that man.

CHORUS
What new catastrophe
Has fallen on the house of Cadmus?

MESSENGER
Death, and one who dwells here cause of it.

CHORUS
Who is the guilty one? And who the victim?

MESSENGER

Haemon is dead and victim of no stranger.

CHORUS

Killed by his father's hand or by his own?

MESSENGER

His own. Driven to it through anger with his father.

CHORUS

Teiresias, mighty prophet, foretold all.
Tell me how and where Haemon came to die.

MESSENGER

Acting as Creon's guide, I led him to
That distant stretch of plain where Polyneices
Lay, his corpse unburied and unpitied,
Mauled by dogs and vultures. We prayed there
To the goddess of the roads, and Pluto
Lord of the underworld, to stay their anger.
And then we washed the body with all ceremony
And burned with wood of fresh-cut olive branches
Those last sad relics of the son of Oedipus.
Finally we raised a mound of earth above them.
We turned next from that tomb, to go where
Antigone has her rock-hewn cave.
Approaching it, the foremost soldiers heard
A voice upraised in violent sobbing. They ran back
To inform Creon, but he had heard it too.
He cried: 'Can what I hear be certain? Is that voice
My son Haemon's? Run forward quickly, guards,
And when you reach the place pass through the gap
At the cave's mouth, and look if it is Haemon
Who weeps, or if some god deceived me.'

[196]

So, with the foremost guards, I ran inside.
Through the dark of the cave's inmost recess
We could discern Antigone's body, hanging
By a cord twisted from fine linen;
And there beside her, Haemon, both arms around
    her,
Crying out in a loud voice,
Railing against her for leaving him to go
Among the shadows, and against his father
And, last, lamenting his own unhappy love.
Creon, drawing near, exclaimed,
'Unhappy boy, what have you done? What madness
Has seized you? Haemon, my son, come to me
Out of the shadows, to me, your father, let me
    embrace you.'
Haemon glared back at him with blood-shot eyes
Then, without a word, spat in his face,
Drew his sword and thrust it against Creon
Who rushed out of the cave. Then Haemon drove it
With all his force through his own side.
With his last breath he clasped Antigone
And dying on their kiss, out of his mouth
A thin-drawn line of blood crossed her white cheek.
Corpse clasping corpse they lay, their marriage rites
Sepulchred by death in the stone cave:
Their deaths bore witness to that evil
The worst known to mankind, insensate arrogance.
Here comes the King, though, bearing in his arms
The fatal consequence of his ill deeds.

(*Enter* CREON, *bearing in his arms the body of* HAEMON.)

CREON

Dark, dark, dark, dark – alas for
Those deeds done in ignorance by me,
Blinded by self-will and arrogance
Weighed down by death with this my heavy burden.
Look on us now, the son
Murdered, the father murderer.
Blind in counsel, blind in all my deeds!
Haemon dead in his youth, his spirit fled
Not through his folly that I blamed but through
No folly but my own.

CHORUS

You learned too late the truth Teiresias taught.

CREON

Too late I've learned
My lesson to the uttermost
End, beyond all new beginning. And yet
I think there must have been some god
Hurled me from the just policies I followed
Down into chaos, the abyss
Of my obdurate cruelty.
Destroying all capacity for joy.

CHORUS

You caused not only your son's death
But, too, that other's – hers.

CREON

Yes, murderer of them both –
Haemon and Antigone, their love.
Lead me away,
Where I can no more see the light,

[198]

Rash fool I was who have slain
My son I loved, his love, and my own joy.
Everything I touched turned to confusion.
Come, blessed day, for me the day
That is my last, where I'll see no tomorrow. O,
    Oedipus,
Blind, blind, blind.

(*He is led away.*)

ABOUT THE AUTHOR

STEPHEN SPENDER was born in 1909. At Oxford he met W. H. Auden and Christopher Isherwood, with whom he was to be instrumental in creating a revolution in English letters. His *Poems* of 1933, published when he was in his early twenties, gained him recognition as a major poet of his generation. After serving in the Spanish Civil War, he worked as an editor of the celebrated magazine *Horizon*, and later on *Encounter*. His autobiography, *World Within World* (1951), was a much-admired achievement in the genre, and he is the author of many other noted works of poetry, drama, criticism, reportage and autobiography. He has taught at University College, London, and at many universities in the United States, and was knighted by Queen Elizabeth in 1982 for his contribution to English literature. Sir Stephen and Lady Spender live in London and in Provence. They have two children.